A Wise,
Blue
Autumn

A Wise, Blue Autumn

A Novel about Fathers, Daughters,
and Remembering

Donald S. Smurthwaite

Author of *Fine Old High Priests*

BOOKCRAFT

SALT LAKE CITY, UTAH

Library of Congress Cataloging-in-Publication Data

Smurthwaite, Donald, 1951-
  A wise, blue autumn : a novel about fathers, daughters, and remembering / Donald S. Smurthwaite.
    p.   cm.
  ISBN 1-57345-922-4
  1. Reminiscing in old age—Fiction.   2. Fathers and daughters—Fiction.   3. Mormon families—Fiction.   4. Aged men—Fiction.
  I. Title.
PS3569.M88 W57   2001
813'.54—dc21   00-050885

Printed in the United States of America   54459-6803
10   9   8   7   6   5   4   3   2

For Cody R. Young (1973–1999)
and Bishop Marc S. Tanner (1950–2000)
both of whom taught much about
having gentle hands
in our wise blue autumns

CHAPTER ONE

I tell stories. I tell stories all the time.

I tell them in the words I choose to describe what I see. But I tell stories in other ways. I tell them by the look on my face, the way I walk, the way I yawn, the way I put down a book on my lap, the way I gaze at photos perched on our piano, the way I stare out our big windows toward the mountains on these short, brisk autumn afternoons. I tell stories when I bend over to plant seeds in my garden come May or when I pull a golf ball from my pocket and gingerly place it high upon a red tee. I tell stories when I reach across the bed at night and pat the hand of my wife, Helen, as I have done for nearly five decades. I tell stories by when and where and how I pray.

In everything I do, I tell stories. I cannot get away from stories. I think it is the way of most people and, perhaps, especially, of Latter-day Saints.

The stories I tell are good stories because they are true to me.

I see stories everywhere, too. In the school children as they walk home and wave and call out, "Hello, Marcus!" I see stories in the young woman at the grocery store holding ground beef in one hand, a roast, perfect for Sunday dinner, in the other. I see stories in the man, my age or more, who waits for the bus at twilight on a busy city street. I see stories when our bishop, bundled against the chill of a winter night, walks alone toward the door of a family that is troubled. I see stories in our deacons, wiggling and mischievous, as they sit through an endless sacrament meeting. I see stories in the heavy eyelids of a baby boy on his mother's lap, fighting off sleep, straining to soak in a little more of his new, curious world.

I see these stories, and they become my truth. I learn from these stories. I see wisdom and courage in them. I see failure, faltering hope, and disappointment. I see encompassing love and bitter anger. I see things that cause my soul to soar and things that are ineffably sorrowful. These stories are all around me. I think they are around us all. They are powerful in their ability to cause us to rise and fall, understand and doubt, love and fear.

Sometimes, I see stories when others would say there is no story to be seen at all.

It is November, a time when the leaves are mottled and mostly fallen, and the first snow only a single icy blast of winter away. Three trees, maples, each tall and gaunt, now almost leafless, stand in our backyard. I have a cold, and my head pounds and feels weighty. I pull a blanket around my shoulders and settle back in an old and friendly chair, and I watch the trees, sniff, and think of when I planted them, now almost thirty years ago.

"Are you feeling any better, Marcus?" Helen calls from the kitchen.

"No, I am not. I want to shake the hand of the man or woman who invents the cure for the common cold, but I do not think I will live long enough to see it happen."

"You will not die from a common cold. Stop worrying. You worry too much. Can I get anything for you?"

"No. I will sit here and be miserable and be just fine at the same time."

"What are you doing?"

"I am staring at the trees in our backyard."

"Those trees. We should have them pruned in the spring. Maybe we should have them taken out. They drop so many leaves. It's hard to keep up with them. They're so big now. You're not as handy with a rake as you used to be, and you're too stubborn to hire someone to clean up the leaves."

"I like big trees. We'll see."

Coming into the room, she looks at me with suspicion. "Are you imagining things about the trees? You have an imagination like none other. You're thinking of those trees, aren't you?"

"I might be." I like to keep a few secrets from Helen, even at age seventy-three, but it is becoming more difficult to do so. "My imagination keeps me young. If I didn't have my imagination, I would be a sickly old man, shriveling up like a raisin before your eyes; and you would be saddled with looking after me, even when things got unpleasant. You would not enjoy that part of life."

"No, I suppose I wouldn't, but I would do so gladly, other than the part about unpleasant work, which I take to mean emptying bedpans."

"My imagination may be all that is separating you from bedpan duty." She turns and walks away toward the kitchen, shaking her head.

"Imaginations are beautiful," I croak, trying to make one last point.

"I suppose they are. You've proven that to me. Marcus, you're funny."

Helen reaches up into a kitchen cupboard. She believes she's already discovered the cure for the common cold—a can of chicken noodle soup. For these fifty years I have known her, every time someone in our family becomes ill, Helen prescribes chicken noodle soup.

Many chickens and many noodles have given their all in the Hathaway family's pitched battles with colds, the flu, chicken pox, mumps, headaches, sprained ankles, and an assortment of bruises and cuts, both physical and emotional.

I have never told Helen this, but I do not like chicken noodle soup. If she prepares some for me, when she is not looking, I will pitch it in the sink.

"I'm fixing you soup, Marcus. I'll set the timer; then you can pour yourself some. You'll feel better if you eat it. I'm going over to Ruth's for a few minutes to check on her."

"You are an angel of mercy," I say. I feel better. Disposing of the chicken noodle soup will be easier than I thought if Helen visits Ruth. I can dump my cup of it into the sink and run water, and she will be happy, thinking the chicken noodle soup is in my stomach when in fact it is on its way to a sludge pond somewhere. My secret of fifty years will be safe. And her wifely pride will be intact. Even when you have lived almost three-quarters of a century, it still feels good to occasionally get away with something. Although I suppose that if chucking out chicken noodle soup when my wife isn't looking is the worst of my sins, I may yet stagger to the finish line and wind up somewhere in the celestial kingdom.

Helen walks to the closet and puts on her coat. "I'll be

at Ruth's for only ten minutes or so. Don't fall asleep and let the soup burn. I wouldn't want to waste that soup."

"Nor would I, dear," I agree.

Ruth lives three houses down from us. She has been a widow now for about eighteen months. We check up on her almost every day. It has to do with a promise I made to her husband, my friend Sam, on a long night in a hospital just before he died. That promise, and a whole lot more.

The door clicks closed, and I turn my throbbing head slightly and look again at the three trees in my backyard. Three trees. Three daughters, Helen and I produced, although I acknowledge she did the vast portion of the hard work.

And on a gray, raw, prewinter day, one that seems to say, "I am the first of many such days to come," I think of gentle spring, two sets of hands joining to plant those trees, and the reason why I will never allow them to be cut down.

I see a story in those trees.

We have been in our new home for only a few weeks. A day of warmth and sunshine, fragrant air and mild breezes is at hand. The daffodils in nearby yards, with their promise of a winter drawing to a close, poke their slender stalks through hardpan ground that was frozen only two weeks ago. Our home looks and smells new and fresh, and Helen has been working long hours to arrange things in it so that all is just right. Now that our marriage seems a good bet to survive not only building the new house but the move itself, Helen is exhausted but pleasantly so.

I have been dutiful, moving furniture wherever I am commanded, hanging pictures, and generally trying to be helpful and handy, while not being too obtrusive as Helen's gone about setting our home in order.

But now that our house is becoming a home and our daughters are feeling comfortable because their things are close by, now that we have actually had a couple of home-cooked meals, I am looking with designs at the large back-yard that slopes away from the house.

It needs trees, I think. *Trees that will grow tall and straight and strong.*

"I am going to the nursery to look for trees," I announce to Helen late one Saturday morning. She is slumped in a chair, her hair pulled back, her shoulders hunched inward. Clearly, fatigue has displaced her uncommon sensibility, and I realize that I can say almost anything at this point, and she will agree. I could say, "I am going to buy a new sports car now," or "I think I will fly to the Caribbean with Sam this afternoon for a round of golf and a late supper," and she probably would smile and say, "That's fine, dear. Could you check the picture you hung in the entryway on your way out? It's crooked."

So I have her right where I want her, which seldom happens in my household. But my designs are modest; I want only to purchase three trees and plant them in my backyard—because we have three daughters and somehow I see that the day will come when my daughters are all away, and I will take small comfort in gazing at the trees planted in their honor.

I like to plant things that will last, which seems to be a good rule not only for trees in yards but for many other things, too.

So I drive to a nursery not far away, and Mr. Jeppesen helps me select three reedy maples that look frail and almost frightened, but the nurseryman assures me they are healthy and much stronger than they appear. He helps me load the trees into my station wagon, and I drive home with them, a journey of triumph. "You will be part of our yard," I say to the trees. "In time, our youngest daughter will climb your branches. You will provide a promise of renewal in the spring, give us shade in the summer, and in the wintertime you will confirm that beauty can be stark as well as effulgent. In the fall, you will remind us with each colorful leaf that trees, and sometimes people, too, are at their best in maturity."

I turn the car into my cul-de-sac and decide that I should no longer talk to the trees, just in case someone overhears and rumors begin circulating in the neighborhood about Mr. Hathaway's mental state. I sneak a glance at the trees in the back of the car, and although it is silly to think it, I imagine they are having good feelings about me—glad to be going to a yard where children and grandchildren will someday swing from their branches and play in their shade, not sent where they would serve as decorations within little islands encircled by concrete in the middle of a strip mall parking lot.

I recruit Kate, our eldest daughter, a senior in high school, to help me unload the trees. Kate is glad to help; like me, she enjoys planting things and watching them grow, and her Saturdays are most happy when she has dirt under her fingernails by sundown. We work for the next two hours, digging three, deep, round holes along the far border of our backyard.

Kate and I grunt and giggle, laugh and lug, and generally have a wonderful time planting the trees across from the big window on the west side of our house.

We are joined by Kate's sisters, Debra and Elizabeth, but they show only a passing curiosity and let it be known that their father has severely disappointed them by concentrating on trees rather than reassembling their swing set. Helen wanders outside for a few minutes, nods approval at our selection of trees and where to plant them, and then goes back into the house, where more chores certainly await her.

By four in the afternoon, the three trees are planted. They stand straight, and happy thoughts of enjoying them for decades drift pleasantly in my mind. Kate is happy, too, and I know it will be another hour or two before she washes the dirt, her badge of honor for the afternoon's work, off her hands. We stand back and look at the three skinny maple trees with a feeling of great satisfaction.

Kate says, "I like these trees. It is starting to look a little bit like a yard now."

I say, "Yes. The trees are beautiful. You know why I bought three, don't you?"

"I do. I will be the middle tree because I would like to think of my sisters on either side of me," she said. And I am both pleased and a little concerned that she reads her father's mind so well.

It seemed like spring then, but it was not. We all got our hopes up when the skies turned a fine deep blue, the cold west winds stopped blowing, and the daffodils and crocuses showed themselves after working their way up through the heavy, wet soil.

As it turned out, it was a false spring, and the temperatures were soon back in the teens, and it snowed three times in one week, and I had to wear my winter coat and gloves and my wool stocking cap to work again. I also had to shovel snow from our driveway, which is probably my least favorite thing to do in the whole world, other than having to go to a day-long meeting on Saturday about the importance of doing missionary work. And as the icy winds whipped them and their thin little branches sagged under a wet heavy snow, I worried about my three trees.

"Are the trees all right?" Kate asked one evening, when the western sky looked like dark gray granite and the wind made a tattering sound as it blew through the rickety, leafless trees.

"I think so. I hope so. We will not let anything bad happen to our trees," I said.

Saturday came, and Kate and I inspected the trees. Two of them seemed to be weathering things fine, but one did not. The middle tree looked droopy and was tilted to one side. Kate had only to look my way for me to tell what she was thinking. *This is my tree, and it doesn't look right. Something is wrong, Daddy. We have to help this tree. We can't let this tree die.*

I said to her, "If the tree is dying because of the cold, there is nothing we can do. The cold has already killed the roots, and without good roots, it won't survive. I'm sorry."

She pulled her long brown hair back around her neck and said, "I'm not sure it's the cold. I think there is an air pocket or something down by the roots."

She studied the tree, then turned and walked into the house. I followed her, and since the weather still wasn't all that pleasant, I was content to be inside. I grabbed a book and sat down in a big chair, pushing aside any thoughts of a dying tree. About ten minutes later, I glanced out the window. There was Kate, shovel in hand, picking at the hard frozen soil. I sighed. I wanted to stay inside, where it was warm, read my book, and let nature take its course with the tree. Then I thought of Kate and how this tree was hers and how I had talked to the trees on the way home and told them they were lucky because they weren't going to end up in a parking lot somewhere. I laid down my book.

I put on wool gloves and my stocking cap and was at her side in minutes. "I thought about it," she said. "It's an air pocket. I'm sure of it, Daddy."

"I'll work the shovel. I suppose the ground is frozen again," I said.

Kate knelt by the tree. When I stopped to rest after loosening a little of the hard, cold soil, she reached with her bare hands to scoop it out of the hole.

We alternated digging and scooping and gradually uncovered the tree's roots. As the hole grew, we felt a sense of urgency. We knew that the roots could not be exposed to the air for very long. My hands grew cold, then numb; after a while my fingers seemed to be nothing more than stubby pieces of stiff wood. I could barely move them, and when I tried to flex them, it was painful. Kate's hands were blue. It was hard, miserable work, and it took us more than an hour to get to the bottom of the tree, and I still couldn't see any air pockets near the roots.

"We need water now," Kate said, and she disappeared into the garage and returned a moment later with a bucket filled to the top. She poured the water into the hole around the tree, and the only way my hands could have become colder was to put them in the mixture of water and mud and tree roots.

Naturally, that's exactly what I did.

I fished around in the dark goop, straightening the tree roots while Kate gradually filled the hole with the soil we had so painstakingly removed. By this time I was a complete mess; my hands frozen, my muddy clothes stiffening, and my face caked with heavy, dried soil. I was tired and a little bit cranky.

And when we were all done, we knelt together on the frigid ground, looking at the little tree. Its appearance hadn't changed much, other than that it stood a little straighter. Part of me was disturbed; more than two hours of work, and my hunch was that it would do no good. The other part of me was pleased; we had given the tree our best help and knew that whatever happened, we would not feel that we had left something undone.

"Well, it's up to you now, little tree," I said, and I didn't mind that my daughter heard me talking to the maple tree.

"Daddy, I think it will be fine. I really do," said Kate, who looked as muddy and miserable as I did. "Thank you. I know it's just a tree. But it's not just any tree."

Over the next few weeks, the weather grew softer. The sunshine came again and invited all that had been locked away in winter's cellar to burst forth and turn green. In early April, we saw buds on two of the maple trees. In the third week of April, buds peered shyly at us from the middle one, and I thought of Kate's faith that the tree would be fine. I have often thought since then that it is foolish to lack faith in anything that is capable of growth.

Our little middle tree grew strong and beautiful, and it has been the first of the three trees to bud every spring. Perhaps difficult starts make things stronger in the end.

So today when Helen talked about trimming the tree or removing it, I could not help recalling how hard Kate and I fought one wintry day to keep the tree alive.

An air pocket. Kate knew that. Kate was right. The cold was not killing the tree. The tree roots were in the wrong element.

And because the middle maple tree has seen our children and grandchildren gather beneath it, because it has provided leafy shade in the summer and brilliant splashy displays on autumn afternoons and endured in stark bareness so many cold, moonlit December nights, the tree will remain as long as I do, and perhaps even longer.

The timer for the chicken noodle soup buzzes, and I slowly rise from my chair and walk to the kitchen. I spoon some of the broth, take a sip, and dump the rest down the disposal. If Helen asks me if I had some soup, I can say yes.

A half hour later, she comes home. All is well with Ruth, she reports, although the faucet in her kitchen sink is leaking, and she wonders if I can look at it, which I will do, of course. She asks me if I had some soup, and I answer that I did, feeling only a twinge of guilt.

She stares a moment at the three maple trees in our backyard.

"I've thought about it, Marcus. I've thought about those three huge maples in our backyard. I guess I don't want them removed. If you can put up with the leaves in the autumn, I'd like to keep them there. They are pretty. And when I look at them, I think of our girls. Three trees, three girls. Maybe I'm just getting old and sentimental. What do you think?"

"I think you are right; I think you are sentimental," I say sleepily while settling back into my big chair. "But being sentimental is one of the good parts of being human."

"And I'd miss the shade in the summer."

"So would I," I mumble.

"Then it's settled? And you'll perhaps hire one of the boys in the ward to rake the leaves next fall?"

"Yes, I'll hire one of the boys. It is settled."

She walks back in the kitchen and scrunches up her nose. "The sink smells like the soup. Are you sure you ate all of it?"

But by that time my eyes are closed, and I think it wiser not to answer but slip again into a gentle, sweet sleep.

My sleep is peaceful, at least until near the end. I begin to wake; I hear the ticking of our mantel clock in the living room. In the muted place between sleep and wakefulness, I hear my heart beating, and my slow, rhythmic breathing. I nap more than I used to. I find it easier to sit still now.

In such times, quiet and restful, I move easily across the seamless line between my dreams and reality. I have certain feelings and hear faint voices, unmistakable yet mostly unintelligible. They are like the sound of gray autumn leaves scuttling across the sidewalk, blown by a wispy, unseen wind, familiar, yet bearing a message about dark, cold days to come.

I think that as I hear the faint voices more, I understand what they say. And what I think they are saying is that a change lies ahead; that my time here is almost over.

Almost over? I am Marcus Hathaway, and it was only a few years ago that I was a child growing up in eastern Oregon. It was mere months ago that I saw a pretty girl with long dark hair and knew immediately that she was the one I would marry. It was only last week that I began my law practice, as unsure and as unsteady as a speckled fawn standing for the first time. It was only yesterday that I held all three of my daughters while my wife snapped a photo with our little instant camera, a portrait that became my favorite of all pictures. It was just a moment ago that I held our first grandchildren in my arms, little twin boys, and thought I had discovered a little of what it means to be a patriarch.

But the leaves rattle by and whisper the same message: "Almost over. Almost over, Marcus Hathaway." And the gray leaves are whisked away from my sight and blown to a new world that I cannot see.

I have known when each calling in my life was coming, and I have also known when each was about to end. Why would it be different for the great calling, life itself?

I do not much like these feelings and voices. But they are undeniable. And maybe it is better to have a warning when such a landmark looms ahead.

Brigham Young once said that thinking of dying is much worse an experience than the actual passage itself. Of course, he was alive when he said it, but I suppose he knew what he was saying. So I try not to think about dying, and try not to think about my withered hands, the dewlaps of skin that hang limply from my face, my pale, swimming gray eyes, and the many other signs that my body is simply wearing down and wearing out.

So I contemplate things that are more pleasant. I think of stories of which I have been a part. I think *What do people say of me? What stories will they tell of me in times yet to come?*

Latter-day Saints know what we can take with us: our wisdom, our knowledge, and our relationships. But what do we leave behind for others to learn from?

Only the stories that are told of us. That is all we really leave. Not our lands or wealth or possessions of any kind. Only our stories. What will my stories be?

I open my eyes and look outdoors. No dry, brittle leaves are in sight. I must have been dreaming, a working dream, where thoughts, some of them hard, have come to me. But something lingers from this dream. I want to know this: What stories will be spoken of me? It is at once a simple and complex question, a life reduced to anecdotes.

I have not sought much in this life, but I now feel a new sense of urgency to acquire something. I want to know the stories that are spoken of me. My friend Sam Nicholson once said that I was the truest of storytellers he had ever known. He told me he loved the stories I told. Is it wrong for me to want to know the stories about me before I leave? Is it wrong to want to know what my legacy will be?

The answer, I think, is no. It is not wrong.

Some people build buildings or contribute money to colleges or donate land for parks as their legacy. As my monument, all I want is to know that the stories told of me are good and true and that I leave behind an unblemished name.

My eyes are open now. I have slept a long while. It is the middle of the afternoon, darker than when my nap began. Jumbo clouds, puffy and dirty white, are blowing in from the west. They will bring the season's first snowfall. The wind that drives the clouds pushes the few remaining autumn leaves across our backyard, blowing them at the feet of the maples. There. No mistake, no dreaming this time. See them? Autumn leaves, scattering and scurrying before a winter wind.

They talk to me.

A clear, strong thought takes shape and form: Find out what those stories are, Marcus. Find out now what they are. I sit up in my chair. I have had a revelation.

I will learn the stories of my life now. I will learn them from those I love the most.

CHAPTER TWO

A day shrouded in low clouds and a wind born of icy, arctic parents, but no snow. I park my car behind a long line of school buses, next to a playground of shaggy brown grass. I tuck my hands deep in my pockets and walk toward the school doors, where a flood of youngsters swirls out and scrambles toward buses and carpools. I walk inside and smile at the school secretary, Diana.

"Hello, Mr. Hathaway. Is it as cold as it looks outside? Your nose is all red."

"It is cold. That wind has teeth. We may have a snow day tomorrow," I say.

"I'm ready. Curling up in front of a fireplace beats coming to work," Diana says cheerfully. "Are you here to see Betsy?"

"I am."

"You know the way. She'll be happy to see you, I'm sure."

I turn to my right and walk down the hallway, navigating around the last little stragglers of the day. I walk to room 3B and glance inside the door. There is my Elizabeth, the youngest of our children, a school teacher now for a decade. She is putting a coat on one of her second-graders, buttoning it to the top, tugging the hood up and over the child's little ears.

"You had the sniffles in class today, Rachel. Let's keep

you warm on the way home. I think it's cold enough to snow," Betsy says, and she gives the girl a little hug.

Rachel turns and sees me. She smiles.

I say, "Hello, Rachel."

She says, "Hello, Marcus."

"How was school today? Was Mrs. Chambers mean, or was she in a good mood?"

"She was in a good mood. She was nice," Rachel says, smiling.

Two weeks ago, it was grandparents' day in Mrs. Chambers's class. I was drafted to be a surrogate grandparent for two little girls and one little boy. Rachel, with dark curls, blue eyes, and a pretty yellow dress, stole my heart as she grasped my hand, then served me overbaked cookies and a sweet, syrupy punch.

I think it is fine to be seventy-three years old and completely under the spell of a seven-year-old with a smile to match tulips in the springtime. I think that even the Father, with worlds and solar systems, universes and galaxies awaiting His beckon and command, still enjoys the feeling of seeing a seven-year-old smiling. I cannot imagine a God of complete love being any different.

"Take care of the sniffles, Rachel. I want you to be well and happy. The sniffles may prevent you from being both, if you aren't careful."

"I will, Marcus. Good-bye!" and she throws her arms around me and gives me a hug before scurrying out the door, where the wind slices from the north like a cold, sharp knife.

"I'm surprised. I didn't know that you were coming by this afternoon," says Betsy, picking up an eraser and waving her arm across the chalkboard.

"A spur-of-the-moment thing. I hadn't planned on it, either."

"What brings you to Mrs. Chambers's second grade classroom?"

"You, most certainly, Betsy."

"Just a social call?" she says, turning away from the chalkboard and looking at me. "Or something else? You have that look in your eye. You are being sneaky about something, Dad. I can tell."

In this way Betsy is very much like her mother. I can hide very little from her. With Betsy, I couldn't even get away with tossing my chicken noodle soup down the drain. She would know. She would make me eat it. Then she would scold me.

I look around the room. On the large bulletin board behind her desk is the November calendar, decorated with paper pilgrims and turkeys, pumpkins and sheaves of wheat, all in place, counting down the days until Thanksgiving.

"Or did you just come here to say hello?"

"No. It is more than that. I do have something on my mind to ask you. A favor."

Betsy has light brown hair, which is brushed back. She is tall and thin, like me. She also has her mother's natural caution. "What is the favor?"

"I would like to hear a story."

She says, "A story? You came here to ask me to tell you a story? I tell stories all day long to my class. This is a true role reversal. My father asks me to tell him a story." She laughs lightly. "What kind of a story? About planes or rockets, magic bicycles, or dolls that come to life? I can tell you many stories."

19

"This is a different kind of story." I pause and glance away. "I would like to hear a story about me."

She pauses and looks at me with serious, hazel eyes. "About you? A story about you?"

"Yes, about me. Some kind of a story about me, or us, or our family. Some story that you would tell to someone else if they asked, 'What is your father like?'"

I feel awkward. I didn't want to have to coax a story from her. I wanted her to tell a story freely, one that came naturally to mind. I wanted her to tell a story about me without her knowing it. Instead, I blurted out my request, and I am embarrassed at my clumsiness. "You know I like stories," I add hopefully.

Betsy turns away from me. She walks over to the long line of windows that face the east in her classroom. She stares at the stunted, mottled grass on the playground, then lowers her head for a moment. The wind doubles its fists and slams the building's windows, then bullies the empty swings. Betsy's silence lasts a dozen heartbeats or more. I have troubled her. I think, *I'll just say, "It's okay. I don't really need a story from you now. It was just something I thought would be nice to hear, but you can tell me one some other time. I am sorry, Betsy."*

Then she turns, and her eyes are moist.

"I'm sorry," I say.

"No. No need to be sorry. But when your parent asks you about a story, and your parent is getting older, . . . and your parent loves stories, and, well . . . you know what I am feeling. I am feeling a lot of things."

I say, "I do." Living with women for fifty years has taught me a few things about the way they think, although I know I am not yet an expert.

"Maybe some other time."

"No. It's okay, Dad. It's okay. The swing sets out

there . . . they're empty. Looking at them, I know a story to tell you. They reminded me of one."

She walks over to her desk and sits down. "Do you know what story I'm going to tell you?"

I nod yes. The swings, the playground, cold winds, and bitter lessons. And a little girl standing at the edge of a playground, alone.

We have built our new home, moved in, and are starting over. Helen is called to serve in the Nursery, and I am asked to work with the Blazer Scouts. We are becoming acquainted with new neighbors, new routes to work, a new grocery store, and a routine that plays to a slightly different melody.

But the starkest changes are those faced by our children. Our eldest, Kate, is at BYU, beginning her freshman year, and we hope feeling a little homesick; Debra is a ninth grader, navigating through the transition to high school; and our little Betsy is making the greatest adjustment of all, beginning kindergarten.

"You will like school. You will meet other little girls, and they will be your friends," I tell Betsy when she crawls in bed at night and stares at the ceiling and asks me sweet, innocent questions about what school is like.

"You will jump rope. You will learn how to read and write a little better. You will be called up by other girls on the phone and asked to attend their birthday parties," I say. I feel wise in my choice of words, in the picture I am painting. A new world awaits her, one of hair ribbons, shiny shoes, friends, books, teachers, songs, and school plays. I describe a kind and gentle world, a place where a little girl will flourish and feel safe and nurtured, caught up in a continual round of fun, friendship, and adventure.

Betsy looks at me. On the nightstand next to her bed is a tablet of paper, and she has drawn pink hearts all across the sheets. Pink hearts are her symbol. She draws them always, everywhere.

"Are you sure, Daddy?"

"Yes, I am sure," I say; then I pull her blankets close to her chin and kiss her on the forehead. "You will like school. I know you will."

I am not alone in painting a glorious picture of days at school. I have my confederates. Kate has primed Betsy with stories of her own happy days in kindergarten. Debra tells her about friendships from her first day of school that still endure. Helen joins in the chorus; she tells our Betsy of joyous recesses, snacks in the cafeteria, room mothers, joining the Blue Bird Girls, and celebrating birthdays with cupcakes and balloons.

"I think I will like school," says Betsy, accepting in her innocence what we have told her. I turn off the lights, and as I move toward the door, pink hearts seem to sparkle and dart in the darkness of her room.

Then the day comes and she begins school and none of our sunny predictions for glory and success come true. Not one. School, it seems, is very different from the happy mural painted by our well-meaning family.

"It was a watch day," says Betsy, the bow in her hair drooping and her black Mary Jane shoes scuffed. "I watched. When I went out to play, I watched the other kids. That's all I did. No one wanted to play with me."

And when she said it, something sank inside of me. My heart ached. Something was wrong, something I could not correct. And I mourned a little, too, for the bit of innocence that had been chipped away, like a flake of paint peeled by a harsh July sun. Then Betsy got her tablet of paper and picked up her favorite drawing pen, a special one that Helen had bought just for her, and she sat down in front of our television set and drew one pink heart after another, as though the pink hearts could turn into balloons that would gently lift her and carry her away.

"I am sorry for our Betsy," I say to Helen that night as we lie in bed, thinking of pink hearts and still smarting from the sting of her rejection.

"It is worse than you thought," Helen says, fluffing up a pillow.

I said, "Worse? How can it be worse?"

She said, "Betsy went up to a group of girls during class time and again at morning recess. She asked them to be her friends." Helen paused. "They told her no."

My Betsy is in pain, and I try to think of something, anything I can do. I suppose these pains are part of being a parent and part of being a child, and perhaps part of any close relationship.

I could see it: Betsy's hopeful, tentative approach; the sting of the snub; the haughtiness of the little girls. Who was the ringleader? How could they be so cruel? How could they reject my Betsy? I felt angry, sick, helpless.

The next day I phoned home early in the afternoon, calculating just when Helen would have had enough time to greet Betsy and ask her how her day had gone.

Helen sighed and her voice was soft. "Another watch day."

And the next day the answer was the same when I called. Yet another day of watching others at play.

"It doesn't make sense, and I feel so helpless," Helen

said to me as I chased the last of the silverware around the sink with one hand, a limp dishrag in the other.

"So do I. That's the worst part of it. I know it will change. I know she will make friends. I know that she won't come home during her junior year in college and say, 'It was a watch day.' But I wish I could help her now."

It was then, just as I grasped the last of our dinner forks and started scrubbing them, that my idea came to me. The idea felt good. It felt right. I was unsure if it was a spiritual experience and the Holy Ghost was giving me a revelation, or if I was just an anxious father wanting to spare his child from pain. I decided it was the first, a concerned patriarch receiving inspiration for his family. I thought, *Marcus Hathaway, you are a wise man and a good father, in tune, and the idea you are about to propose will put an end to Betsy's watch days.*

I looked at Helen, who was wiping the table clean, and said, "I have an idea, Helen. I think it is a good one and you will like it. I believe it will help Betsy."

Helen gave me a look that seemed to say, "What you are about to say will be a very male answer, and it will do no good whatsoever for our Betsy, but I will hear you out because I know how you get when you are excited."

I decided to ignore her look. "Do you want to hear my idea?"

She said, "I suppose," but without much enthusiasm, and for a moment I imagined myself one of the prophets, sharing some great and wondrous truth with my wife and having her say, "Oh that's nice, dear. I'm sure the Twelve will be excited. Now, would you mind taking out the trash?"

Nevertheless, I forged on.

"This is my idea, Helen." I paused for dramatic effect.

"Whirlytwirlies."

She looked at me for a few moments, sheer puzzlement on her face. "Dear, you will need to explain that one to me."

"Whirlytwirlies," I repeated. "What I have done in the backyard for many years with our daughters—where I take them by the wrist and they run in a circle until they are airborne. Then I twirl them around and they laugh and giggle—"

"And become sick to their stomachs."

"No. I want to go to Betsy's school and perform whirlytwirlies. I will make the little girls laugh, and they will think Betsy's dad is okay and cool, and they will want to be around her on the chance that her father will come by and do whirlytwirlies again. I know it is a crude plan, but I think it will work."

She smiled at me, a patronizing smile. "Marcus, you are a kind man, and I will love you always; but whirlytwirlies will not make an ounce of difference to our Betsy. Oh, you may have fun, and they may have fun, but it won't make any lasting changes. It is too complicated a problem to solve by tossing little girls into the air and making them dizzy."

"Well, I would like to try. It can't hurt," I said, finishing the last of the silverware. I looked outside. It was cooling off now in the evenings; frost would soon visit, and with its icy nimble fingers begin the work of pinching off leaves and sending them toward the ground. "It can't hurt," I repeated.

Helen leaned over and put some freshly cleaned plates on a nearby shelf. "It won't work," she said a few minutes later, as she yawned. Then she walked to the sink and rubbed my back playfully. "But try it. You wouldn't be my Marcus Hathaway if you didn't."

And so it was that I found my way to the playground the following morning, a day that seemed more like summer than fall, when the sun, tired and old from its hard August work, nevertheless found the strength to toss a few, last, warm, lazy rays into our world. I explained to the secretary, a woman wearing a dubious look coupled with glasses with heavy, dark frames, that I was there at the invitation of my daughter and that I wanted to visit her in her room. The school secretary sized me up thoroughly, evaluating the chances that I might have some other, more sinister motive for being there.

"It's recess time," she said. "Your daughter is not in class at the moment." She pulled on a golden, dangling earring and seemed to think the matter settled.

I, however, thought this a stroke of good fortune. I have learned from my experience as an attorney to take an opponent's best argument and turn it against him, and I have learned to do so deftly, with a few quick words, and at that moment I thought that perhaps law school had not been a total waste of time after all. I smiled at Mrs. Bigframes and said, "Perfect. I will just go to the playground and watch her there," and before she could raise a hand or utter an objection, I brushed by her and through the door to find my Betsy.

I stood on the crest of a small rise between the school and playground. Before me dozens of children played and cavorted, as though to the frenzied violin of a Paganini caprice. I turned to my right, and there stood Betsy by herself, a few feet away from the swing set.

Quietly I walked to her. "Betsy. Hello."

She turned, looked surprised, then smiled and threw her arms around me. Pink hearts were all I could see.

"I came to play with you. I was nearby and thought I would see how you and this old school are getting along."

She said, "Everything is fine, Daddy. I just don't feel like playing with anyone right now. I just want to watch."

"But would you play with me if I asked?"

She turned her head quickly, looked at the other children nearby, jump ropes in hands, legs kicking high at the apex of the swing set arc, chasing big yellow or red rubber balls around the playground, and came to her decision quickly.

"Yes. We can play."

"Whirlytwirlies?"

She looked pleased. No one else on the playground could do whirlytwirlies.

"Come with me, over on the grass. If we crash land, I want you to be on the grass, not the asphalt."

I took off my suit coat and hung it on the monkey bars and stuffed my necktie into my pocket. Betsy held her hands out to me, and at first I took them gently; then I locked my fingers around hers. Her eyes widened, and she started to run in a clockwise direction. Our momentum grew, and she kicked her feet skyward; she was airborne, hand-to-hand with me, at a perfect balance point between gravity and centrifuge.

She giggled, and her world and my world dissolved into a dizzying blur.

And for some reason, I thought of our daughter Kate, whom we had just dropped off at college, and how I now held the young one in my hands as we spun madly on the school yard. And I hoped there was a way always to hold onto my daughters no matter the forces that tried to pull them away, and I wondered if Betsy's swaying ponytail really beckoned others to come and play, or if it was the first wave good-bye to her father.

We twirled for a half-minute while play ceased on other parts of the playground. It was unusual for an adult to be there in the morning, and even more unusual for one with a suit on to be splitting the air with a little girl. A curious crowd gathered, and within moments of stopping, we heard the shouts: "Can you do that to me? Can I go next?"

I obliged as many as I could in the next quarter hour, before recess ended. Betsy, our watch girl, was now surrounded by other children, who were begging her father to whirlytwirl them. I gleamed with perspiration, my stomach felt as though it were filled with sweet, sickly gelatin, and my arms ached. But it was worth it. Betsy was happy in the midst of other little girls and boys. Assuredly, this would be no watch day. There would be no more watch days for Betsy ever again.

A bell clanged, and the children bounced their way back to class. Betsy walked in with girls on either side of her, all smiles, chattering happily, and all I could see when I looked at her were pink hearts.

"You can't believe how well it went," I told Helen that night, as she thumbed through her scriptures after dinner. "And you doubted. You said it wouldn't help. Betsy could be elected kindergarten class president tomorrow, she's so popular."

"Perhaps you were right, dear," Helen murmured, but I thought her voice lacked conviction. I wanted her to call me wise and loving. I wanted her to acknowledge my genius in understanding how humanity works. I wanted her to praise me for so neatly solving Betsy's problem.

"But we'll see how tomorrow goes. We prove everything

in our tomorrows, you know, nothing in our days past. Endure to the end, Marcus." She pushed her funny little reading glasses lower on her nose. Clearly, my genius would go unrecognized this night in the Hathaway household. Helen yawned. "Where is that scripture that Brother Sanders quoted in Gospel Doctrine last week? The one about Paul saying all things are pure unto the pure?"

The next day was long. I fussed and fidgeted, alternately brooded and felt euphoric. I could hardly wait to get home that afternoon and ask my Betsy about her day. Surely it had been successful. Surely she had jumped rope, played tag, had her pick of peers to balance on the teeter-totter. Surely all that and more had happened.

She was at the kitchen table when I got home. Helen was in another part of the house. My heart pounded as I saw Betsy. She was drawing huge pink hearts, her little face a study in concentration, her small fingers tight on the crayon. I approached her cautiously. I could barely speak the words to her.

"How was school today?"

She didn't raise her head. In a soft, flat voice, she said, "Oh, it was a watch day."

"It can't hurt," I had told her mother two nights before, so sure, so confident, so willing to do what I thought best for my child. *It can't hurt,* I had thought. I was wrong. It did hurt. And it hurt very much. Oh, how it hurt.

That night I did all the things that a father should have done with Betsy. We played a game of checkers. I read her a story. Helen and I said prayers with her, tucked her into bed, and kissed her cheek. And I hoped that somehow, where a father's plan to twirl his daughter to acceptance had failed, that some other miracle, unseen and unknown, would nevertheless take place and all would be well for

Betsy at school. What I had neglected to realize is that anything that twirls eventually wobbles; then, it must fall down.

The evening was a roll of fine satin, tinged with bronze at the edges by a setting sun. I sat on the steps in front of my house. My neighbor Sam walked toward me, bouncing a golf ball on the sidewalk. I thought he did not see me, but as he drew perpendicular to the porch, he stopped, turned toward me, and took off his funny old fishing hat.

"Good evenin' to you, Mr. Hathaway."

"Hello, Sam."

He plopped his golf ball down twice on the concrete, its click making a satisfying sound. "So, are you going to tell me what the matter is, or allow me to guess?"

"How do you know when something isn't right?"

Sam put his hat back on, took a step forward, then leaned in my direction. "No clues at all. Just that it's nine in the evening, almost dark, and you're sitting on your front porch looking as though President Kennedy just called you up and asked you what he ought to do with Cuba. Your head is buried in your hands, you've added a couple of impressive lines to your face since I saw you on Sunday, and you're scowling."

He bounced the golf ball again. "Marcus, you never scowl. Nope, no clues tonight." He looked skyward, where Venus, cold, blue, and distant, was peeping over the southwestern skyline. "My guess is that it's your kids."

"Sometimes you amaze me, Sam. You are uncannily wise. You are right. It is Betsy and her first week at school. It sounds silly, but I want her to be liked, and so far she is not. She stands by herself and stares while the other kids play. She calls them watch days. This is kindergarten, Sam. It should be different. Why are things so difficult?"

Sam plinked the golf ball to the cement three more times.

He smiled. "We want our children's lives to be a calm ocean, with only occasional gentle swells and fair winds, don't we? But it isn't that way. At most, we can provide them a harbor where they can ride out the storms and feel safe. Betsy needs her harbor and she has her harbor and she knows it. Kids with no harbors are the ones we should worry about. I see them all day long at school."

I envisioned boats bobbing on a swollen ocean for a moment, each with a name painted on its side, then said, "I think you're right about harbors. Betsy does have her harbor. You are almost always right. You unnerve me sometimes by always being right. You and Ruth are the most perfect people I know. Sometimes, it makes me feel ill."

He said, "Hogwash. Let's play golf. I will shank a few shots, mumble words that are not polite, and toss my wedge into the air at least once. You will know then that I am far from being perfect. Besides, people should try to be good first and perfect later."

I said, "The golf game is a deal. Short afternoon at work tomorrow. We can sneak in nine holes if we tee it up by five. I will feel better on the golf course, especially if I'm on top of my game. There is something therapeutic about smacking a golf ball."

He bounced the ball three more times and said, "See you then, partner. And she will be all right. Remember, she has her harbor." Then he threw the golf ball down hard on the sidewalk, and it bounced high into the air. He took a step forward and put his hand behind his back. The ball came down squarely in his palm. He doffed his hat and whistled as he walked away.

I miss Sam. I miss his hat. I miss his silly golf ball tricks. And I miss his advice.

He was right, of course. Betsy did gradually make friends in kindergarten. She did get invited to some birthday parties and was even asked to join the Blue Bird Girls. We heard about watch days for a while longer, but we paid less attention to them and more to making sure that our Betsy knew, always knew, a safe harbor was as close as the walls of her home. Now, almost thirty years later, I think she still knows that.

"So you remember whirlytwirlies and kindergarten days and trying to make new friends?" I asked.

"Yes. And even then, when I was five years old, I saw through you. I knew you didn't just happen by to see how I was doing. I knew you came to school because you loved me," Betsy said.

She stood up and walked to her chalkboard. She picked up an eraser and made wide, swooping motions with it.

I said, "This is the story you will tell then?"

And she answered, "It is one of the stories I will tell." And I could not see her face, but her voice was low and hoarse, and I wondered if she also heard the leaves rustling and understood what their whispers meant.

Outside, a crack appeared in the moody, flat-bellied clouds. A slender stalk of sunshine sliced through them. For a moment, and only a moment, the march of coming winter is stalled. I look toward the swing set. A young man is there, pushing a little girl forward against the cold wind.

I cannot tell if the scene is real or exists only in my imagination.

CHAPTER THREE

I was wrong about the coming weather. Snow never appeared that evening or night; in fact, the lumbering gray clouds blew away during the high tide of darkness, leaving a pale, frigid sky in its place. The bony hand of late autumn touched the earth and coated everything in a deep layer of steely frost. The world I awoke to looked cold and aloof and seemed to say, "Do not attempt to become part of me today. I have no energy, no time, and no warmth for you or anyone."

Helen caught up with me a little later, after I had dressed and gone to the kitchen for breakfast.

She yawned and said, "It looks so cold outside. I don't think the furnace ever stopped running last night. A good morning to stay inside, I think," and I was impressed that she read the mood of the day exactly as I had. "Are you feeling any better, Marcus?"

"Yes, I am. My throat is no longer sore, and my head doesn't feel stuffy."

"It must have been the chicken noodle soup I fixed for you yesterday."

"Yes, it must have been. Thank you. I salute the chicken and the noodles who gave their all for the soup. It went for a good cause, namely, the perpetuation of Marcus Hathaway's earthly existence."

Helen giggled and ran her hand through her long hair.

"A good cause indeed. I've watched Ruth for a while now, and I would prefer not joining the ranks of the widows at any time in the near future."

She walked over to the round oak table where we ate most of our meals. I was hunched over a small bowl, earnestly working to garner on my spoon the last couple of fugitive corn flakes floating in a puddle of milk.

"Remember, freezing outside or not, Ruth and I are going to the grocery store this morning. We thought about maybe shopping a little after that. Would you like to come?"

I did not want to go, although accompanying Helen to the grocery store might allow me to sneak back to the shelves the several cans of chicken noodle soup most certainly on her shopping list. When her cart got good and full, and when she looked away, I could snitch the cans and put them back on the soup aisle. I thought, too, of Brigham Young, a man whom I respect and revere, and wondered if any of his dozens of wives ever asked him to go shopping. I suppose they did, and I suppose when they did, he would merely invoke the air of a man who had other important business and quickly decline the invitation. I tried to do the same with Helen, by standing up and by trying to summon a look of seriousness and dignity, which is difficult to do when you are holding a spoon with two corn flakes in one hand and you are wearing a faint milk mustache, as I was. "No thanks, dear. I have other matters to attend to."

Helen looked dubious, because most seventy-three-year-old men have little to do on frigid mornings, much less "other matters" to attend to, unless, for example, you happen to be a member of the First Presidency or Quorum of the Twelve, a thought that had obviously never occurred to the Lord concerning me.

And if by some chance the thought had occurred to Him, I'm sure He had smiled and had Himself a gentle laugh.

"What kind of matters?"

"I thought I might drive to Debra's. I haven't seen her for a couple of weeks. She said she had some old photos she wanted me to look at. It's too cold for anything else, other than shopping in a nice warm mall."

"Well, okay, but you are passing up the opportunity to be with two attractive women for most of an entire morning," she said.

"A fact of which I am well aware, but age brings equal measures of wisdom and foolishness," I said. "My choice manifests the foolishness part of the equation."

I said this to Helen but was really hoping to look at photos and hear another story.

So it was that I drove my way to Debra's house a half-hour later. She lives in a large home in a newer neighborhood in the foothills north of our town. It is an impressive house, with two large columns in the front and a sloping yard that is always green in the summer and cared for by men who speak Spanish and work hard in the hot August sun. From the tall windows on the east side of her home, the mountains seem close enough to hold in the cup of my hand. The driveway is long and curved, leading to a garage that can house four cars. In the backyard is a swimming pool, drained and covered at this time of the year. Debra; her husband, Quinn; and their three children built the home three years ago, and I can remember the pool being used only once or twice.

Her home is in perfect order, meticulously clean, organized, a place where no common speck of dust would dare drop and settle. I sometimes think I would feel more comfortable in her home if there were some dust to be seen and a few toys scattered on the entry floor. I once, with all the strength of character I could muster, resisted the temptation to run a hand coated with chocolate birthday cake frosting across one of the white walls in the family room.

I parked and walked to Debra's front porch. A puff of icy north wind sent a shiver through me. Two maple leaves, wizened and blotched, scurried by my old brown shoes. I rang the doorbell and Debra answered. She is tall, slim, and graceful, and through an unaccounted left-hand turn of genetics, is blonde-haired and blue-eyed, defying her mother's Italian ancestry and my own coloration scheme of brown and gray.

"Hi, Dad. I didn't know you were coming this morning," she said.

"Nor did I. My choices were a trip to the shopping center or visiting my daughter. It was an easy decision to make."

"You made the right choice. Come in. I'm just getting Andrea off to school. I'll be with you in a moment."

In the back of the house, I saw Andrea, her youngest child, bundled in a heavy red coat and purple pants, scuttling toward the back door.

"Hello, Grandpa!" she shouted at me.

"And hello back to you, Andy."

"Got your lunch?" Debra asked. "Got your homework? Remember the book?"

"Yes, I do. I'm okay, Mom."

"Good-bye, dear," and Debra leaned over and gave her a kiss, then closed the door behind her.

Debra walked back into the living room, where I had taken a chair.

"What's up, Dad?"

I said, "You mentioned pictures. Some old photos that I should see."

"Oh, yes! Those. I found them in a box that had been placed way back in the utility room closet. They must be twenty-five years old. I'm not sure how I even got them."

"Old photos are like old friends," I said, then added a bit slyly, "every one of them tells a story."

Debra looked distracted. She pushed back a wisp of her hair and smiled faintly. "I suppose they do. You of all people should know. The king of storytellers."

"Maybe. I have told many stories, and most of them are true. And in my mind, I guess I think all of them are true." I decided, with the instincts of a used-car salesman, to go for the close. "How about you, Debra? Do you have stories? Do you have a story about me, for instance?"

She glanced quickly away. Like Betsy, she was surprised. The notion of telling a story to a parent was foreign and unexpected. "You want to hear a story about yourself? That's not like you, Daddy. I can't tell stories the way you do."

I said, "I have told many stories, but almost all of them are about other people. I thought it might be fun to hear a story about me. Like a photographer who has his photo taken for a change. Or something like that."

"Something like that," she said, with a sigh. "I suppose I could tell you a story, though I'm unsure why you want to hear one." She crossed her legs and used her left hand to pull her long hair back off her forehead. "Okay. Okay. I think I have one, but don't expect it to be told in the tradition of the masters, like the way you and Brother Nicholson could."

"I will not. It is, after all, the feeling of the story, not the way it is told."

Her blue eyes were now bright, her hair seemed to be spun of fine strands of gold. It felt good to see Debra, our least outgoing and most private child, to be excited about a story. She sat forward in her chair.

"It's not really much. Only a little story, but something I will always recall. Do you remember the district cross-country race my senior year?"

The district cross-country championship. Do I remember? Of course I do, of course I do.

A cool, late October Thursday, damp from a storm that blew across the Pacific, dropped its cargo of rain on the Cascades, and retained just enough moisture to coat our part of the earth with a fine, wet sheen.

Rain fell on downed leaves, making them slippery and treacherous.

And it was the day of the district cross-country race. Debra, lithe and agile, with the quiet determination of a pioneer mother, was our runner.

"Will you be at the race, Daddy? It's district. We have a chance at winning. Then we'd go to state. I hope you can come."

"I will be there. I should be there. I haven't missed many of your races. I love to watch you run," I said. I purposely had booked a light afternoon at the office and was confident I could go. Helen could not. Betsy had the flu, and Helen thought she might be coming down with it, too, so the responsibility of being the Hathaway family cheerleader fell directly on my shoulders.

And I wanted to be there because I learned something about life every time I went to one of Debra's races. She was a good runner, but not great. She ran that year as the fifth seed from her school on the cross-country team.

I always thought Debra ran with her heart more than her legs. She hardly ever ran fast, and rarely ran slow, but always kept close to the same, steady pace, a style that does not win many races but does get you to the finish line, something that counts for a lot in cross-country running.

Anyway, one of my clients came in for a two o'clock appointment, and he was distraught: his business was failing and his creditors were starting to get nasty with him, and his marriage wasn't going very well, and his teenaged son was giving him fits, too. On top of it all, he was a Church member, and I was doing a lot of listening and giving him about equal doses of legal and spiritual advice. Then I looked at my watch. It was 3:30, and I needed to be on the other side of town in a half hour for the race. I was faced with one of those "dad choices," where I wondered if I should be a good Christian and listen some more while this emotionally disheveled brother poured out his heart to me or if I should excuse myself and get to the cross-country race.

I gave him another few minutes, but when he started getting into some areas that I thought his bishop should hear about rather than his attorney, I was happy to suggest that he make an appointment with Bishop Nicholson and work out a few things with him. He seemed to think that was a fine idea, and I felt wise and good and not at all guilty about setting up Sam, because taking on the woes of your congregation is part of the bishop's calling, too, although you'll never find it written in the *Handbook of Instructions* in quite that way.

Anyway, the brother stood up and shook my hand, and I smiled and wished him luck and reminded him to schedule an appointment for the following week. As he closed the door, I ran to the hat rack in my office; grabbed my heavy winter coat; told my secretary, Miss Seibert, that I was leaving for the day; and drove a little too fast to the golf course where the race was to be held.

The day was nasty, indeed—the sky nettlesome and dark and the day-long drizzle now turning into a serious cold rain. Not many good parking spots were left, and I had to wedge my car into a narrow slot between a pickup truck and a fire hydrant three blocks from the golf course. I slammed my car door, hurried to the course, and had just caught sight of the runners bunched at the starting line when the starter's gun sounded. Debra had gone off without my support and was now somewhere in that writhing tangle of arms and legs and ponytails, running down a long fairway.

I was disappointed. I felt as though I had let her down because I hadn't been there in time to see her off and wish her luck and maybe give her a quick kiss.

I have always liked cross-country races because they have so much to do with what I believe in: hard work, endurance, courage, and introspection. I ran a lot in high school, and I know how difficult it is to sprint to the finish line, when your arms feel as though they each weigh one hundred pounds and your lungs burn as though hot lava was in them and your legs feel like long strands of wet pasta. It is at moments like that when the introspection begins and you think, *I can't do this. I can't do this. . . . I better get started and do this.*

I have no proof of this. It is just a feeling, but I believe that many of the prophets were probably good runners. Samuel the Lamanite, for example, must have been in pretty good shape to scale the walls of Zarahemla, call an angry citizenry to repentance, and then get the dickens out of there without anyone catching up with him. And after he secured the plates of Laban, I imagine Nephi didn't just stroll away from Jerusalem but probably sped away, sandals flying, dust arching in a long, dusky plume.

In vain I searched the pack for Debra's long thin legs and the swaying tail of her pulled-back hair, but most of the runners were already around a corner on the first hole. It somehow seemed important that she know that her father was there. I knew the golf course, and I half-walked, half-ran toward the sixth hole, high on a hill, where I was sure the course would take them. The runners did come by, straining, pale, and puffing, but Debra was all the way across the fairway, and although I let out a shout of encouragement, my words fell unheard to the wet, brown-green grass.

My stomach started to tie itself in knots, and I felt the sure prickle of panic inside. Only one place remained where I might see her: the long narrow fairway of the ninth hole, a straight shot to the finish line. Again I scurried toward the place where I hoped to see my daughter.

It is interesting how much we do and give to see our children as we get older. We will drive long distances for a glimpse, travel in the dead of winter to attend a school play, and sprint across a golf course, dressed in a suit, splattering mud, panting, to shout encouragement to a child in pain.

The first few runners came down and around a hill and then spilled onto the fairway, amidst cheers and cackles. I didn't expect to see Debra among the leaders, and she was not. More runners came; still my daughter was not to be seen.

Twenty runners went by, then thirty. Debra, I thought,

must be laboring. She must not have it today. She must be struggling. She must be in pain. How I wished I could run this last part of the course with her, but I knew I could not.

Finally I saw her come around the corner, and my instincts had been right. She was in pain, her stride weak, her skin wintry and gray. She came from the grove of pine trees, angled down the slope of the hill, tripped on a root, struggled briefly for balance, and then sprawled headlong onto a graveled golf-cart path.

I found myself running toward her, shouting, "Debra! Debra! It's me! Debra, I'm here!" What a sight it must have been, a cold rainy day, a man dressed in a business suit sprinting in his black brogue shoes, his raincoat ruffled and flying, hand in the air, his voice thick with emotion, his white shirt splashed and muddy, and tears in his eyes.

Debra pushed up on her hands, her elbows and knees bloodied, surprised to see me running toward her. I reached her and helped her stand as the other runners plodded by. Someone approached us, a man carrying a clipboard, looking annoyed and sounding pompous. "You can't do that," he huffed, making a note of Debra's number. "What you've done is wrong. She's disqualified," he said.

I glared at him. "No. What I have done is assist my daughter. And I can do that. And the only thing wrong here is what you just said to me." Then, for good measure, I added, "Bub." He stomped off, agitated and fuming, convinced it was more important to follow rules than do the right thing.

"I want to finish, even if I am disqualified," Debra said, fighting back her tears.

I said, "Can you? You're going to need stitches. That's quite a gash on your left knee."

She said, "I can. I want to. Even if I'm disqualified. But I might need help."

And through her tears, grimacing because of the pain, and with blood dripping from both of her knees, she took my arm and hopped and hobbled, gimped and limped her way to the finish line. Debra finished dead last and finished first all at the same time, and I have never since felt so much like a champion.

You learn the most about runners and people when the end of the race is at hand, I think, not at the beginning. As Debra hobbled across the finish line, the spectators cheered her and shouted encouragement. I saw mothers and fathers whose eyes were as wet as my daughter's as she finished the race. Her teammates were all there waiting for her, and not one of them seemed upset that her stumble probably cost them a chance to go to the state meet. They didn't seem to mind.

My eyes and thoughts came back from the wet hillside and knees pocked with gravel to Debra's large, clean home with its curved driveway and useless swimming pool.

She looked at me. "When you weren't there, I worried. I wanted to know where my father was. I really wanted you to come and watch me run. It turned out to be my last race."

"Yes, it was. But you finished as a champion."

She was quiet for a moment, then said, "You need to know something. I never told you this, but I ran in high school only because you loved to watch me so much. You came to almost every race. That's the only reason I ran. I actually hated running."

The irony of that made me smile. I said, "You're kidding. The only reason I came is because I thought you enjoyed running so much, and I wanted to be there for you."

She lowered her head, and I could not tell if she was laughing or crying or just thinking. It is always an awkward moment for a man when a woman, even his wife or daughter, might be laughing or might be crying, and he has the vague but steady suspicion that he is the cause.

"We are a fine pair," I said. "You ran because I enjoyed watching you. I watched you because I thought you enjoyed running."

"We should have had this conversation twenty years ago," she said. She lifted her head, and I could see that I was right on both counts—her eyes were damp, but she was also smiling. "I still have scarred knees," she said.

She stood. "I'll get those old photos now."

I said, "Thank you for running."

She said, "Thank you for coming to my races."

She left the room, and I looked outside. The sun was veiled in high, wispy clouds, its rays feeble, barely able to cast a shadow, the wind now whipping from the west. Debra had no trees in her front yard, but I could not help noticing leaves, more leaves than when I arrived, dancing and beckoning across her lawn, an unseen hand pushing them toward a yet unknown destination.

CHAPTER FOUR

I arrived at an empty house an hour later. The photos that Debra had found were only a dozen years old, a roll that I had taken of smiling grandchildren with their young parents, at a family vacation at a cabin we had rented in the mountains.

I spread the photos out on a table so that Helen would see them as soon as she arrived home. When you are old, photographs bring out the best of emotions and feelings, little records that often say so much more than words. But they can also bring an uneasiness that borders on despair, reminding you of places and times, and most of all people, who cannot be visited again.

One photo showed our three daughters, standing at a boat dock with the blue waters of a lake behind them. Kate looks confident and happy; Betsy, the social one, seems to look beyond the camera lens, searching for someone along the shore behind me. Debra stares straight ahead, a glimmer of a smile.

My daughters. Are they truly mine or are they not? It is a question that after seventy-three years, I still do not know the answer to. I suppose they are, and I suppose they are not. I know what the gospel teaches on the subject in a general way, but I do not know the details. When these thoughts come to me, I often feel as though I am hiking across a high desert plateau, and a huge, deep canyon blocks my route, and I can go no farther, but must walk parallel to the canyon, in hope of finding a safe way down and a safe way up, so that my journey can continue. I am selfish in this respect; I want our daughters to be ours forever, with no deep canyons in my way.

I look again at the photos. "Experience. That is what you all have given me," I say to the people in the photos. "Experience and love, and the chance to gain wisdom, and to feel in ways that I never would have known otherwise. I think we can never underestimate the value of experience in this life," I ramble on to those featured in the photos. "In the next life, we will probably sit in many councils, and we will talk and teach one another. And we will recount our experiences and share them with one another, and the stories we tell will be as gold to us. And although our experiences came at a cost, such a high cost at times, a cost that we didn't even comprehend, we will long for the days on earth again, when the fine mixture of faith and experiences came so easily and so often and our opportunities to learn were endless. That is what we will miss about our life on earth, I think."

As I grow older, I find myself talking to inanimate objects more and more. Photos. Books. Furniture. Cars. Houses. It is one of the secret pleasures of age. So far, none of them have talked back to me, but I have no doubt that day is coming, too.

I settle in my big chair and glance out the window toward the three trees in my backyard, their bare tops swaying in the stiff fall breeze, nodding back and forth, as if agreeing with my thoughts. And I recall a talk I had with Sam once, on a fine day late in October. I close my eyes for a moment, and it seems as if my friend is nearby and our words as fresh as if spoken yesterday.

Autumn though it was, good weather graced our earth for a few more days, about a week after Debra fell at her cross-country meet. The day was surprisingly warm, and the sun shone a bright yellow in its cozy sea of deep blue. The forecast for good weather was supposed to hold through the weekend.

Sam and I knew exactly what a gift such as this required. He called me at work during his lunch break on Friday and said, "It would almost be a sin to not play golf on Saturday. I do not want to sin. I have sinned too many times already. My salvation may be imperiled."

"I do not wish for you to sin, either, Brother. I do not wish for your salvation to be put in peril. Heaven has given us the gift of an unusually favorable Saturday. We are told to recognize His hand in all things. It would be a sin of omission to not recognize a beautiful day such as this. The golf course would be a fine place to revere such a mild and good day. I have had moments of unmistakable spirituality on the golf course, at least three or four occasions, through the years. Playing golf tomorrow is not only a good thing to do, it seems the right thing to do. I'll pick you up at seven."

So we ended up on the golf course, and even with the beauty around me, I did not have a good day hitting the ball. I was trying to break in new shoes, and they pinched and blistered my feet, and by the eleventh hole, I was in unrelenting pain and my whole day was close to turning into a devastating emotional experience.

Why I could not get a goofy little dimpled ball to go where I wanted it to was one of life's great mysteries that day. When I wanted it to go straight, it went crooked; when

I wanted it to go long, it went short, when I wanted it to be sweet and simple and obedient, it was mean-spirited, complicated, and self-willed.

Playing golf is good preparation for rearing teenagers, I believe. The complexity of the game and the discipline it demands is yet another witness to me that golf is a type of heavenly pursuit and that the game will be played in life hereafter.

Anyway, when a man is having a bad day on the golf course, he has two choices: he can get frustrated and angry and brood, or he can get philosophical, which for some reason, seems more difficult to do than throw a temper tantrum.

That day I took the high road and was getting philosophical. It is a consolation, of sorts, if you can say to yourself, "Maybe the golf ball is winning today, but at least I'm acting like an adult."

Sam and I had just played the fourteenth hole, a long par five, more than 500 yards from tee to cup. "What did you get on that one, partner?" asked Sam, who was keeping score.

I knew I had three-putted, which in golf is a cardinal though common sin—a silly and wholly needless folly, but one that happens occasionally nonetheless. I had dubbed my second shot on the fairway but wondered if it should really count as a stroke since it had rolled only about twenty feet. I had also chunked a chip shot and had finally reached the green in five. I added it all up and concluded that I had made an eight. But hoping Sam would show some compassion, or better yet, that he had not noticed all my pitiful shots, I reported, "Seven."

He dutifully wrote down my score, which, a few minutes later, I happened to look at and see that he had scribbled an "eight." Golf, I suppose, should be like life, ending in a perfect judgment.

Anyway, I was limping badly, and Sam finally said, "Your new shoes bothering you? You're walking as if your foot is broken."

"Yes, I have blisters, certainly," I said. Then, thinking of Debra and the gravel in her knees, and the red, angry blisters on my feet, I decided to impress Sam with my philosophical bent, although just swearing might have been easier and more satisfying.

"I am also distracted," I said. "I keep thinking about Debra falling down during that cross-country race and how painful it must have been. She had worked so hard, and it was a disappointing and inglorious way to end her high school cross-country career."

I knew that Sam knew about the ignominious race because I had overheard Helen telling Ruth about it on the phone, and I could tell Ruth was saying many sympathetic things to her, and I was sort of expecting the same from Sam. I might have even hoped that when he got home and Ruth asked how the round went, he would say, "I did just fine, but poor old Marcus had a miserable day. He was worried so much about Debra." Mormons, I believe, enjoy imagining conversations among others in which they are portrayed as great mothers and fathers, as priesthood leaders without peer, and as having that sixth sense about when a chicken and cheese casserole or a plate of cookies is needed to the point where it might actually turn someone around.

We like to imagine someone standing at the doorway with tears pooling in his or her eyes, accepting the casserole dish with deep-felt gratitude and blurting, "How did you know? Thank you, thank you! I've been such a bad person. But I see the error of my ways, and I know I need to repent. I will schedule an appointment with the bishop right away, and I owe it all to your wonderful casserole."

Well, that kind of sentiment and sympathetic touch was what I was hoping for, but Sam didn't deliver it. Instead he stood up on the next tee and whacked his drive down the middle of the fairway. Feeling a little overlooked and a trifle miffed, I rose on my sore feet and somehow managed to duplicate Sam's shot. We trudged down the fairway, the dark jade of Scotch pine tree branches waving in a gentle wind as if to greet us, and I had the vague but undeniable suspicion that Sam was about to make a point with me.

We reached his ball first, and he took out his four iron and sighted in on the flag, a little more than 200 yards away. He took his precise, taut swing, and launched the ball on a low, boring arc. It landed about 25 yards short of the green, took a couple of hops, then rolled up close to the pin. It was a very fine shot indeed, and I was impressed by his ability to concentrate on golf when his friend was suffering so and practically begging for his attention.

I couldn't resist making one more attempt to obtain a little brotherly comfort. As I said before, my game that day was simply awful, and being philosophical seemed to be the best way to salvage some dignity.

"It was sure tough on Debra, and it was tough on her dad, too," I said as we approached my Titleist, sitting up nicely in the middle of a pale green fairway.

Sam looked at me benevolently, and my hope began to rise that he would say something like, "You are a wonderful father, and yes, that must have been tough for both of you."

Instead, he said, "How many stitches did Debra take in her knee?"

I said, "Six. And her other knee was really scraped up."

"All pock marked with little rocks?"

"Yes. We had to pull some out with tweezers."

We arrived at my ball, and Sam stood back a respectful distance as I settled in over my shot, then returned to my form of that day, topping my ball. It rolled weakly ahead of us, stopping a good distance away from the green, and I uttered what must have been my fifteenth, "Aw, nuts," which is what I always say after the golf ball has once again made me feel foolish and insignificant. *Here I am,* I thought, *a human being with divine origins and part of a royal generation, and this little round object can make me feel as though my existence is pointless and my life a failure.* I thought, *Maybe you've over-rated this game. Perhaps it is a telestial activity. Then again, beautiful things can be made to look ugly, and you, Marcus Hathaway, are doing a fine job of turning the beautiful game of golf into something tawdry and mundane.*

We ambled toward the green, and I chipped my next shot to within a dozen feet of the hole. I was eager to resume my conversation with Sam.

"Six stitches and gravel in her knee," I repeated.

Sam had his putter in hand, and he looked at me with a trace of annoyance.

"Seems like a cheap price to me."

I was startled, so I said, "What is a cheap price?"

He said, "What did you and Debra learn when she fell down?"

I thought for a moment. "Well, I suppose she learned something about finishing. Something about getting up when you are down. She probably learned something about enduring to the end."

"Is that all? Those are the answers I would expect of an average man."

I had covered the basics, but it was obvious that Sam wanted to go deeper into the subject. I thought hard, which is not the easiest thing to do when you are having a bad day on the golf course.

"I learned that I will do anything for my daughter," I finally said.

"Good. And what else?"

Sam was in his full mode as a schoolteacher now, but I did not mind because I needed the education. I had, indeed, almost invited it. And besides, I thought I had come up with the right answer, and I did not want him to call me "average" again.

"Debra. She learned that same lesson . . . that her father would do almost anything for her. I think she has heard me say a million times that I love her, but it is the things we do that show our love. My feeling for her was shown by running across that grassy fairway in the rain and helping her when she needed it. That's what you mean, isn't it, Sam?"

He conjured a look of supreme satisfaction. "Yes, that is what I mean. Not to sound harsh, Marcus, and not to take away the pain of your daughter, and not to diminish your own emotional agitation, but six stitches and scraped knees is not a steep price to pay for such knowledge. Now, I have a chance to birdie this hole, and that would give me a great deal of satisfaction, so please allow me to putt." Then, as he lined up his putt, he added, "She will remember what happened at that race on that golf course for the rest of her life."

And so she has. And I know more now about what Moses meant when he wished that every person were a prophet. We all can be prophets, I believe, in our own appointed way. It happens naturally, when we are in tune and our wisdom flourishes.

Brigham Young said that we could live a thousand years and we would still have experiences each day that would teach us and bring us closer to God. Sometimes I like my experiences and sometimes I don't, which, I suppose, makes me like almost every other mortal rambling around on the earth. Mormons should value experience more than anyone else, because we know that to gain experience is one of the big reasons we come here. And besides, we all agreed to the deal, although I'm not sure any of us really understood fully all that was included in the package when we raised our hand to the square and said we'd go to earth and follow the program. Maybe it was better for us that way.

"Go to earth? You bet. Experience physical pain? No problem. See loved ones suffer? I can do that. Watch as those you care for stray? I can handle that." In our innocence we may have said all these things and more.

Perhaps it is this fine and beautiful blend of experience and wisdom that causes me to like stories so much. Every story represents experience, and every experience brings us closer to walking in the footsteps of God.

Anyway, what wisdom I have has come through experiences. Maybe it is because I am an old man and have too much time on my hands, but sometimes I worry that people, and especially Latter-day Saints, have experiences all the time but don't seem to learn much from them. If we can't find meaning within our experiences, or at least have the smarts to wonder what the meaning is, we're missing the whole point.

On Judgment Day, when we appear before the Lord and He asks how things went here and the best we can do is say, "Well, I don't know, I guess things were pretty good," I think He might contemplate sending us back until we get it right.

Through the years I have expressed my views on experience and meaning and learning and wisdom to Helen. She usually listens patiently, and she agrees with me up to a point; but I remember one night about five years ago, when we were talking before falling asleep, and she said, "Marcus, you are the most Mormon man I've ever known. Only you could find deep spiritual meaning and wisdom in the way Brother Allison conducted opening exercises in priesthood meeting."

Maybe she was right, but I would rather be guilty of trying to see too much spiritually than be surrounded by ministering angels and never have a clue.

In the middle of these pleasant thoughts, I hear a jumble of keys and the squeak of the front door opening. I hear the voices of Helen and Ruth and know the shopping trip is over. The sky is still darkening; my thoughts turn to the possibility of snow. And while I cannot hear them scraping against the walkway to my house, or hear their crinkly edges scuttling across my driveway, I look at the few remaining leaves on my three trees and see a few more flutter earthward.

CHAPTER FIVE

This time Nature behaves and delivers on the promise of yesterday's sky. First light, and pearl-gray clouds, low, brooding, and heavy, a skyward Mahler symphony accompanied by a whining, cutting wind, spit little icy flakes across our city.

First snow. As most go, it isn't much of a snow; the flakes hurl themselves at the tall windows on the west side of our house, plinking against the pane. It is only a snow of inconvenience—just enough to cause another layer of clothing to be worn, enough to snarl traffic a little, not nearly enough to accumulate in inches. The snow shovel in the corner of my garage, on furlough since the end of March, will be idle yet another day.

"Are you feeling well enough to go?" asks Helen.

"Yes. I think I am over whatever ailed me two days ago. It must have been the chicken soup," I say, and then, looking outside, I add, "I am needed on the job today."

When you are old, the feeling of being needed, of being essential, of having a purpose do not come as naturally as when children were at home, careers on the rise, and the requisites of church service more demanding. It is a challenge of mine, to feel needed at seventy-something.

I took being needed for granted for so many years. I thought it would never end. Now, I know better. I understand that I must find ways to serve, to help others, to make myself useful and productive. Each school-day morning all of this comes into focus as I perform a duty of great magnitude and consequence: I am a school crossing safety guard.

Helen was skeptical at first. "That means every morning and every afternoon. You can't miss. It's such a commitment, Marcus. When the weather turns cold, your joints will ache, and your fingers will grow stiff and painful. The school can find others. The school can find someone . . ." she hesitates and searches for the right word.

"Younger?" I prompt.

"Well, maybe."

"But I like this idea. I like seeing young faces and talking to innocent children. I like seeing little girls in new shoes on their way to school. I like the idea of talking with little boys about their heroics on the playground. I like the idea of helping them cross to safety. I like seeing the sweet mothers escorting their children to the crossing. I like to think of them waking their children up, dressing them, preparing breakfast for them, so that they can have a good day at school. Crosswalk guards do an important work. And when the law school alumni magazine sends the questionnaire about what I am doing, I can write that I am working in educational administration."

"Oh, Marcus. You really are impossible sometimes."

And with that, I knew I had won this round. When Helen says, "Oh, Marcus," it means that she realizes that my mind is set and that she cannot deter me and that she might as well concede defeat. I was a gracious victor. I gave her a kiss and said, "Thank you, Helen. I will be a good crossing guard. I will take my responsibilities seriously."

So since early September, I have been walking daily the four blocks to the intersection of Harding and Powell

Streets, wearing my orange vest and carrying a big red stop sign and generally becoming acquainted with and endearing myself to the younger generation. I endear myself to them by giving them candy and advice. The candy comes only after seeking their mother's permission, and only in the afternoon, so that they will not get into trouble for eating it in class. The advice comes free, at any time.

"You have a new scarf, Abbie. Your grandmother must be in town. Tell your grandmother you love her and that she is important to you. Keep the scarf always."

"Only missed two on your spelling test, Timothy? Wonderful, indeed. You are a smart boy. Next time I think you can get them all right. You will go far in life."

"You look sad today, Sarah. It is okay. All of us are sad sometimes. You will have a better day tomorrow. If someone hurt your feelings, then do not let it bother you because hurt feelings always go away, if you let them."

"Michael, if you want to be an astronaut, then I know you will achieve it. I will look for your face in the moon and stars someday."

And, of course, the children all tell me stories, though they probably never recognize them as such. The little girl, a third grader, who has only three school outfits, but is always clean and well mannered. A boy in fifth grade who rarely says anything, staring silently at the world around him with cold, dark eyes. Another little boy, a second grader, who looks at me one day and simply blurts out, "Do you know that I don't have a daddy?"

The Reilly twins, who love to confuse me by telling me one is the other and then laugh all the way across the street after pulling yet another prank on old Marcus the crossing guard.

A word of encouragement, a hug when needed, a Life

Saver when appropriate, an adult who will listen to them. Yes, it is an important work and a beautiful work—helping these children cross to a safer place. All children need crossing guards. And Helen thinks all I do is walk into the street and hold up my big stop sign and shoo the children across.

At the end of my duties that morning, a sleek, white car pulls up to the curb. A pretty woman rolls down her window and beckons to me.

"You are the best crossing guard in the world," she says, laughing. "And kind of cute, too."

I say, "Thank you. I hope my work is acceptable. And by the way, you're kind of cute also."

She says, "Would you like me to give you a ride home? I might even stop and buy you a cinnamon roll and some hot chocolate, if that would entice you."

I say, "Well, many years ago, when I was a young boy, my mother told me to beware of girls who offered me gifts. I was also told to never accept rides home with anyone except my parents or trusted friends."

She says, "I just would like to take you home so that you could be a grandfather to my children."

I say, "Excuse me, young lady, but I think I already am."

Debra laughs. "Get in, Dad. Let me drive you home. The roll and hot chocolate offer is still good, though. And I want to talk with you. I've been thinking of stories. I have another one that I think I need to tell you."

I say, "Okay. You have made an irresistible offer. I might be able to say no to hot chocolate on a cold day, and I might be able to pass on the cinnamon roll, but when you throw a story into the formula, I am putty in your hands. You know me too well, Debra."

Soon we are in a bakery, seated at a table in a corner, a cinnamon roll between us, two cups of rich hot chocolate sending a fragrant, steamy plume upward. Debra picks at her part of the cinnamon roll; I attack my side of it with gusto.

"A nice surprise you've planned. I need to call your mother, though. She will worry. Especially if someone calls and tells her that I was last seen climbing into the car of a younger woman."

"I took care of that. I called her on my cell phone. She knows where we are and whom you are with. So you won't be able to tease her about it," says Debra, aimlessly stirring her hot chocolate with a spoon.

"You've been thinking. You said you had another story to tell me."

Debra pushes a wisp of her hair away from her face. Now she looks at me intently. I sense that this is a story she needs to tell me as much as I need to hear it.

"I do. But . . ." she hesitates, and I can see she is trying to decide if she should share her thoughts with me. She takes in a deep breath and exhales, then seems resolved as she continues, "But must all stories be happy and have good endings? Do all stories need to end?" she asks. "I feel silly. I feel like a little girl again, asking you at bedtime how the story you're reading to me is going to end. I wish I knew. I don't."

I say nothing to her for a few moments as a worried look passes over her features, clouding the beauty of her face. Then I say, "No. Not all stories have good endings. Not all stories end. Some just go on and on. Some only get better gradually over a long time."

"But it feels so awkward when the stories are that way. Remember, we're Mormons. Everything always works out.

Everyone should be happy. Everything should have a meaning to it that is clear and simple and bolsters our faith."

I say to her, "No. It really isn't always that way. We work hard to make all endings happy, we pray about it, we care, we cry, we try, we wonder, we listen to conference talks and schedule appointments with the bishop. And still in the end, we find an answer that to us as mortals might seem dissatisfying. Some stories do have happy and sweet endings and are beautiful to hear. But some do not. We seldom hear those in sacrament meeting. Life is more complicated than that. Father in Heaven wants us to grow more by giving us a variety of experiences, probably along the order of what He once went through Himself."

Debra sits back, leaving the rest of the cinnamon roll for me. "Still my dad. Still gives the best advice around. Still knows what to say and do at just the right time."

"Well, I try. Sometimes the magic works. Sometimes the magic of being a dad doesn't. I feel lucky today."

She says to me, "Okay. You've earned your story. But it has no ending. Just a conclusion, and that perhaps temporary. It is happy in some ways and sad in others. I won't tell you anything you don't know. It has to do with a princess who lives in a castle and who breaks her foot when she drops a can of applesauce. Is it a story you know?"

I reach across the table and take her hands in mine. "Yes. It is a story I know."

Debra and Quinn were married on a windy morning in May, when the sky overhead was blue but on the western horizon, oily dark clouds hovered. When I left the temple,

I shivered in the bite of a jagged west wind and pulled the collar of my overcoat high against my neck.

All is well, I reminded myself. A new eternal family has been created. When Debra and Quinn knelt across the altar from one another and looked into the mirrors, the possibilities and eternities seemed endless.

And yet, something gnawed. Something didn't seem right. Something didn't *feel* right.

I watched Quinn emerge from the temple doors, crisp in his black and white tuxedo. A handsome returned missionary, from a family of excellent standing. Referring to Quinn Rogers, people always said the same things about him: He will make his mark in the world. Quinn Rogers will succeed.

Our friends, who knew Quinn better than we, often pulled us aside when his interest in our Debra became known. They would say, "You are so fortunate that Quinn is falling in love with Debra." And Helen and I would feel awkward and not know how to answer. Most often we smiled politely and said little, although once, at a high priests social, when the suggestion was made with more presumption than usual, Helen replied tautly, "Well, *we* think Quinn is the lucky one. Excuse us. We need some water. We must go."

And so Debra and Quinn were married, and Quinn set out to conquer the world. And he did a pretty good job of it, at least the corner of it where he settled, and the prophecies about him began to become true, as his name and income grew in our community.

And sometimes I would ask Debra, "How is married life?" And she would say, "Oh, just fine," and never anything more.

But the feelings never left me. I felt unsettled about

Debra and Quinn, and so did Helen. We would talk at night.

"So how do you think Debra is doing?" I'd ask.

"I think they're fine. You worry too much, Marcus." But I would hear the reservation in her voice.

"But I mean *really*, how is she doing?"

And Helen would pause, then say, "I think she is lonely and miserable, and that Quinn treats her as one of his finest possessions." And what followed would be a near-sleepless night, harsh, angry winds of concern making rags of the fabric of our lives. Thinking about Debra and her full but empty life, I became a witness to what I had always heard from parents of married children: You never stop worrying about your children and their problems, no matter how old your children are and how small or large their problems are. It comes with being a parent.

Sometimes I think it would be easier if our feelings were not so fine-tuned, especially when it comes to our children. If that were the case, I could have watched Debra and her husband and their children move to nicer homes, drive nicer cars, take expensive trips and thought, "All is well." Certainly, I would have slept better, and Helen, too. When people began mentioning Quinn as a possible candidate for elected office, I would have felt familial pride instead of a jagged, red concern.

But that is not the way things work. Those darned old feelings. Brigham Young taught that if we were in tune, the Holy Ghost would pour out answers to us like water being poured on the ground, and not a Sunday would go by that we didn't have the mysteries of life resolved. While it is always good to be in tune and to be where you want to be spiritually, it seems to me that sometimes it is not always pleasant or easy. I remember when I served as bishop and would see someone in church, and the Holy Ghost would say, "Better get Sister Rivers in for an appointment. You know what the problem is. And it's not going to be very much fun to work through it with her, but you must."

And I wonder about the Holy Ghost and what He feels, especially when He has some tough news to deliver or needs to work us over a little bit to help us become better. His job is not an easy one, I imagine, particularly when He is trying to get the message across that a son or daughter is struggling.

Quinn continued his upward march, racking up one achievement after another and making money—lots of money. As I worried about his priorities, I often thought that a life is amiss when counting things other than blessings brings contentment. And Quinn had become very good at counting things.

I became more direct in my occasional questions to Debra.

"Are you happy?" I asked once, as we sat on the edge of an alpine lake, her feet and mine dangling in the cool water at the end of a dock, while the sun colored the mountains to the east in shades of springtime roses. There, just the two of us, no one else to hear, I thought she might say something different than all of her usual pat answers.

She did pause that one time, and looked longingly at the rosy mountains, as if she wished for other places and other destinations. But this is the young woman who finished long races when both knees were bleeding and she needed stitches. She was a woman forged, in part, of cold blue ice. Finally she said, "Yes. I'm happy. Who wouldn't be? I have everything."

Yet her voice was flat, and she seemed to be reciting an

answer that she had rehearsed in private many times before.

And at that moment, the Holy Ghost told me something about people who do not feel important in the lives of those who should cherish them the most. What I learned is that it ruins self-esteem, it takes away vitality, and it leaves you feeling unfulfilled and desolate, like a parched desert landscape raked by blowing dust and hot winds. I could see it. Though she couldn't or wouldn't admit it, Debra was empty and lonely.

And I knew that in some mysterious, yet real and terrifying way, we were in danger of losing our Debra. She was on the verge of giving up. She would live her life robot-like, uncomplaining, but forever wondering if there weren't more to it than what she had experienced.

I became angry with Quinn at that moment. He was taking away the vital breath of my daughter, because she was invisible to him. Helen was right. Just another possession among his many. Just another thing to be counted.

I sat there with my feet in the water, and I gently took Debra's hand. I thought of what the Savior taught, about where your heart is, there also will be your treasure. And I thought of the promises in the Doctrine and Covenants that imply whatever we want to become, we will become; the choice is ours, for good or bad.

Quinn wanted to be rich. And he was. And his relationship with work was more important to him than his relationship with anything or anyone else.

He knew more about making money than he did about his own wife.

Holding Debra's hand at the lake, I could only wait for her to speak. Long seconds went by, but it could have been a lifetime, and in a way, perhaps it was. Finally, she pulled her hand out of my grasp and smiled at me from a million miles away and said demurely, "Really, Dad. Everything is fine."

I wondered then, as I had many times before and many times since, if I should sit down and talk with Quinn and tell him a few things about himself that he might not necessarily enjoy hearing. But I always concluded that there would be a better time and that I needed to wait for the Holy Ghost to give me a polite shove when that time came.

I felt that we came so close to finally talking about it that day on the lake. For a moment I thought that Debra would look at me and say, "I need some help. I'm not sure about this life of mine. I didn't think it would turn out this way at all. Is there something better?"

So all I could do was wait. Helen and I, we waited and waited, and watched as our daughter went through the motions of living.

It was near the end of March, mid-morning of a day that couldn't make up its mind whether it wanted to be part of a dying winter or cast its lot with a new spring. One hour it was dark and spitting snow; another, the sunshine soothed the earth with a warm and gentle hand. Helen was at the temple with Ruth. Sam, then alive, had drawn baby-sitting duty for some of his grandchildren. I was recently retired from my law practice and still trying to figure out the rhythm of a day not dictated by the drumbeat of work at the office. I had just about decided to walk to the Nicholsons and offer my help in keeping the grandchildren in tow when the phone rang.

I picked up the receiver, and the voice was Debra's.

"Daddy," she said, and there was a pause, and I knew my daughter of blue ice needed me, was calling as she tumbled down the wet slope in a long and difficult race.

"Daddy," she said again, and I could hear the pain in her voice.

I said, "Debra? What is wrong? Something is wrong."

She said, "I hurt."

I said, "What happened, honey? Tell me."

She said, "I dropped a can of applesauce on my foot. I think I broke a bone. It hurts, Daddy."

Long imbued with the patriarchal sense of order, I said, "Have you called Quinn? Can he take you to the emergency room?"

"I called him at work. He was in a meeting. They got him out, but he said I should be able to take care of it. He said it was only my foot. He sounded upset with me." She fell silent for a moment, then said, "Can you come and help me?"

There is not a father anywhere who can hear that tone of voice in one of his sons or daughters and not respond. I said, "Sit down and get some ice on your foot. I'll be right over."

But I knew that it really wasn't her foot that was causing her anguish.

I hurried upstairs and sat on the edge of our bed. I thought, *This is what you have been waiting for. You must be wise, and you must be careful, Marcus.*

Yes, you don't much care for Quinn in many ways, but he must not become the enemy here. A little assistance from the Holy Ghost would be helpful along about now.

That was not the first time I had cast my eyes heavenward and said in effect, "Excuse me, Lord, but I could use a little help. This is a big one, and I'm not sure I can muddle my way through it on my own. I need inspiration."

I have thought, uttered, and pled with words such as those many times, particularly when I served as a bishop.

My experience is that sometimes He sends inspiration and sometimes He just lets us find our way through, with only an occasional gentle nudge, and it is not until the crisis has passed and we look back that we can see His guiding hand. I once heard that most often we pass *through* trials and not *around* them, and what we should ask for is the strength to keep moving ahead, not to have the trial taken away.

Well, in this case, He might have looked down on me and said to Himself, "Yes, this is one of those times that I need to send a little inspiration to fine old Brother Hathaway because I'm not quite sure he can figure it out on his own."

What I thought of next was pure inspiration and became the lever I used to pry open the rusted door to Debra's life and let the light back in.

I saw my old eight-millimeter movie projector and a box next to it filled with family films. And I knew what I had to do.

I picked up the projector and the box with the little plastic reels of film, put them in the car, and drove to Debra's large house on the hill. This time I did not knock but pushed open the front door. Debra was sitting on the couch, her leg propped up on some pillows, with a bag of ice resting on top of her left foot. I put the box of home movies and the projector on the kitchen table.

"How are you feeling?"

Debra had obviously been crying, and she didn't even bother to wipe at the tears on her cheeks.

"Oh, Daddy, I am so miserable," and I knew she was talking about more than her throbbing foot. "Is this all there is? Is there more? I need to know. Everything is so hollow. I am going through the motions. I don't want to do that, especially with my kids. I worry about them most of all."

"First things first. We need to get you to a doctor. Then we will talk about other things. You will be my captive audience. I have much to say, but I will listen, too."

So we went to the doctor, who luckily wasn't very busy, and he ordered an x-ray, and sure enough, the can of applesauce had snapped a little bone on the top of Debra's foot, and when we got back two hours later, she had a pair of crutches and a soft cast midway up her ankle.

I called Helen, but she was not home yet, so I left a message and asked her to come to Debra's house because she had broken her foot, but everything was going to be okay. I helped Debra back over to the couch and got her comfortable.

"Now, I have a treat for you, Debra. This is something that will surprise you. I have brought our home movies, and I am going to show them to you, and because your foot is broken, you cannot run away."

She looked at me, and I could tell that she was thinking, *My foot may be broken, but Dad's mind must be completely gone.* "We haven't watched those in years," she said. "Are you sure? Why?"

"I think it's important. Trust me."

She shrugged her shoulders and winced from the pain in her foot. "Okay."

I closed the curtains and set up the projector and began to put the reels of film on. Years before I had labeled all of the movies: "Our Trip to Canada." "Hello, Betsy." "Kate Goes to the Prom," which I once used to blackmail her later in her life. But that day I picked out all the films that had to do with Debra. And what flickered onto the white wall that I used for a screen was more than eight-millimeter film; it was the story of a life, a good life, and it reminded Debra of things about herself that she had long ago forgotten.

At one point I heard her say, "I was a cute little girl."

And later, "I remember that bicycle."

Next, "We have a good family. We had fun together."

And still later, and most profoundly, "That's who I am."

And when I turned on the lights once to change the reel of film, I glanced at my daughter, and tears were running down her face, and I realized that the young woman of cold-chiseled ice had become that way because it was the only way she could cope with a life that was sad and lonely and filled with doubt, not because that was who she truly is. Now, that life was melting away in a pool of warm tears. My daughter was coming back. I thought then and have often thought since, *Too many people in our LDS society are lonely and trapped and can't remember who they are. It is one thing to sing "I Am a Child of God" and another to believe it. We seem to lose the meaning of that beautiful, sweet song as the long years wear us down and our lives become too complicated and frayed and we let other people and other things define us.*

I heard a car crawl up the driveway. Helen came in, and she could see something unusual was happening, and perhaps because she had just been to the temple and was sensitive to things spiritual, she tuned right in to what was taking place. After a quick hello and a check on Debra's foot, she said, "Well, the kids will be home in another half hour. Let's watch some more movies."

And I thought, *You have married a remarkable woman, Marcus Hathaway.*

So we watched more home movies, and we all laughed, and we all cried, and we remembered who we were then because it really does have a direct bearing on the people we are now. And I thought, *It is not quite this simple but not much more complicated than this: Life is an interconnected set of circles, not a long, straight pathway.*

And I had long awaited the little shove from the Holy Ghost that told me, "Marcus, you need to talk with Quinn." Sitting there with my wife and our daughter, He put a warm hand on my shoulder and said, "Now is the time, my friend. I will work with Quinn beforehand, and he will understand what you say."

So a day later, I muscled my way onto Quinn's calendar and scheduled an appointment, and we had our talk, and I am pleased to say the Holy Ghost did His part well, and I got through my part just fine. Before I talked with Quinn, I read Doctrine and Covenants section 121 many times, particularly the part about persuasion, long-suffering, gentleness and meekness and love unfeigned, and I think I *instructed* Quinn and did not *reprove* him, which it seems to me is the way the Lord wants us to approach tender situations.

In fact, in all my years of church service, I have tried never to reprove with sharpness, at least not the way most people interpret it; and since I've made it this far, I don't plan to be sharp with anyone because being sharp doesn't feel connected to being wise and humble, two qualities I would like to possess someday. Sometimes I have seen well-intentioned people justify a curtness and cutting spirit in their church duties and family duties by protesting they are only "reproving with sharpness," when an arm around the shoulder and a kind word would have gone a lot further in really helping out.

Well, Quinn and I had our talk, and things began to change a bit. The marriage is still far from ideal, but I am hopeful, and Debra seems happier, and she and Quinn spend more time together, and that old Latter-day Saint guidepost of feelings tells me they are headed in a good direction. Direction is everything in our personal lives. I've always maintained that it is better to be close to hell and marching away than miles from there and walking toward it. I think I read that once; perhaps it was something Brigham Young wrote. It certainly sounds like something he would say.

And I hope to see the day when the Rogers's swimming pool is used and the sparkling white walls of their home are smudged a bit by happy little fingerprints.

So Debra and I sat with our cinnamon roll and hot chocolate in the bakery, and she was smiling.

"Home movies. When I saw you bring in the projector, I thought you had lost it," Debra said, stirring her hot chocolate. "I thought you didn't understand me or what I was going through."

I said, "I did understand. I don't always understand, but in this case, I did, perhaps more clearly than you. Your mother felt it also. Parents are parents forever, and we always want to help, and we will always love you. Those two things will never change, which is how Heavenly Father intended it."

We stood up and put on our coats. "So those are my stories to you, about you," Debra said. "I should write them down."

"Yes, you should. Thank you for the stories. We will make other stories together. We will tell them often. Maybe we will watch home movies again."

Outside, the clouds had lifted some. To the north the mountains were draped in a dazzling sheen of white snow. This was probably the first of the snow that would last, finding a home among our mountains until the warm sun of May would finally melt the flakes and they would slip

71

CHAPTER SIX

Saturday morning comes, and I lie awake, somewhere between the time when the night steals away and first light reaches with long, slender fingers into our valley. Beside me, Helen is asleep, her breathing peaceful, rhythmic.

Not too many years ago, I would have been up by now. Even on a gray November day, when the grass has long ago lost its green luster, and the trees look more like brown, standing forks, their prongs reaching into a cold sky, I would have been hoisting my golf clubs into the back of our car, waiting for Sam to come by.

All those years we played golf, and I always drove on Saturday morning. It was never anything we talked about; it just happened.

We would bundle up against the cold, our pockets warm from our small, kerosene hand-heaters, shivering our way through the morning hours, looking skyward for any signs of snow that might bring a reluctant halt to our game.

In his almost sixty years of golf, Sam had two holes-in-one. The second came on a day just such as this. An almost empty golf course, a sky overhead threatening snow, a wind that thrashed and twisted, a time and a place where no normal men should have been, but I have come to believe that the mere act of picking up a golf club disqualifies you from being considered absolutely normal. It really is a silly game.

I replayed his shot. A par three, of course, 163 yards, a sand bunker on the left, long scraggly rough to the right. Sam pulled his four iron out and lofted the golf ball straight and true for the pin. It bounced a good twenty yards from the hole, and then like an obedient soldier, followed Sam's coaxing right into the hole.

"Did you see that, Marcus? Did you see that! Whoopee! An ace!" And he danced a little dance right there on the tee.

With all the strength of character I could muster, I looked back at him and deadpanned, "See what, Sam? I think you caught the bunker on the left."

The memory of the flickering moment of disbelief on his face brings me satisfaction to this day. Then he must have seen the corners of my mouth curling because he let out another whoop and danced again. I said, "Congratulations, partner. This only proves that beautiful things can happen even on days that are not."

I have played golf for more than forty years now and never had a hole-in-one. I am unsure why; I have lived an honorable life, tried to be a true friend and good husband and father. I would like the Lord to bless me in this regard. I would like to make a hole-in-one while still a mortal. Should there be golf in the next life—and I am firm in my conviction there will be—I don't think a hole-in-one will be as noteworthy because by then we will all be close to perfecting our game. It seems doubtful to me that the Lord will want beings around Him who make triple bogeys and say things that are not appropriate in the celestial kingdom. Therefore, the value of a hole-in-one will be diminished in the next life, I am afraid. Like repenting, playing golf is something best done on earth.

I was lost in these pleasant, early morning thoughts when Helen stirred and reached out and rubbed my right arm. "Good morning," she said to me, as she has for almost fifty years. And when she says it, I think, *Her voice is that of a young woman again. She sounds just like a girl again.*

"Plans for today?" I ask.

"Not much. A little running around. Can you fix Ruth's leaky faucet?"

"Yes. I found my plumber's wrench last night, and I will go over to her house."

"Don't break anything. If it is too complicated, leave it alone. I know you have many fine qualities, Marcus, but you are no mechanic. Nor are you a plumber."

"I know my limitations, and they are considerable. You have my word."

Ninety minutes later, I stood next to Ruth, and we examined her pipe and sink. It appeared to be a simple job, just remove the cap and tighten a couple of screws, something that even I could do. I didn't even need my big plumber's wrench, and I was a little disappointed because carrying it around made me feel more important.

So after I fixed her faucet, I said, "Mind if I climb under the sink and take a look? I have my big plumber's wrench here, and it would be a shame not to take a glance underneath. Just in case."

Ruth said, "No, that would be fine, Marcus. Be careful under there. Do you need a light?"

I said, "No thanks. I'll just take a look."

I climbed under her sink and began to look around.

Ruth patiently stood by.

"Marcus, are you still writing your stories?"

"Yes, I am. I am not sure if I am a good writer, but I like to write stories."

"Why is that?"

I laid my big plumber's wrench down and thought for a moment. It is not easy to be on your back, under a sink, in the dark, with a big wrench, and feel very profound.

But sometimes good thoughts come in dark places, and this was one of those rare occasions.

I said, "I still don't understand this world all around me. When I hear and write stories, it helps me make sense of things and helps me see more than might be there. It helps me organize my life." I paused, waiting for her response. None came forth. So I said, "Is that dumb?"

I heard her giggle in the light above me. It is good when older people still giggle. "No, Marcus. That is not dumb. I think it is wonderful. You are almost three-quarters of a century old and not quite sure what to make of this life. That is laudable, not laughable. I don't know what to say about this life, either. Other than it has been fairly interesting."

"You shared most of your life with a pretty good story-teller, Ruth. Sam could make me laugh so hard I would cry, and cry so hard I would laugh."

"Yes, he could." Then she was silent, and I fussed around under the sink, feeling around for leaks. "Nothing in here. Everything is fine," I said, coming back to the light.

"I was just thinking of a story he told. Just thinking of it today." Ruth was smiling, her head tilted up, and it was clear she had not heard anything I had just said. She was thinking of her Sam instead.

I sensed a story coming, one that needed no coaxing to tell. A bonus story, if I were involved in it. I suggested gently, "Which story? Will you tell it to me?"

"Yes. Yes, I will. You're part of it, Marcus."

"Then tell me the story."

"Certainly. Of course I will, Marcus. It has to do with you and Sam and a cold night in the mountains. Do you know what story it is?"

Yes. I know that story well.

Sam had been bishop for about two years, and though he was as fine a bishop as I ever knew, I could see that serving had been something of a drain on him. The time of the year was July; his son Rob would be home from his mission to Argentina in a couple more months; and yet Sam was sagging.

This is not a phenomenon limited to our Bishop Nicholson, I have decided. Bishops are busy, everyone knows that. What no one knows are the burdens a bishop carries around and how they sometimes weigh him down, how he prays for wisdom and hopes it comes early enough to be useful. And he cannot tell anyone, anyone, that is, except the Lord, what his thoughts are and the weight he feels. We ask so much of our bishops, we expect them all to have a big red "S" painted somewhere on their chest, and yet they really are mostly just okay, normal guys who have a huge responsibility, and if they are a bishop worth their salt, most of the time they are a little awed, a little overwhelmed, a little worried, overly stressed, and always fatigued because of all that happens when you have the worries, sins, joys, hopes, ambitions, and problems of about 500 people pinned to you.

I remember once when I was a bishop, and I had a rare night off. No visits, no interviews, no activities, and the missionaries didn't ask me to do a split. I celebrated by going to the hardware store and purchasing a new snow shovel, trying not to feel guilty because I wasn't out working to save someone somewhere.

While there, I ran into a couple from the ward. They greeted me warmly but with a curious look on their faces. Finally, the sister asked, half-seriously, "So, Bishop. Why are you here tonight? Shouldn't you be doing something for someone?"

And I thought about her question for a second, fought off the guilt, and then said kindly, "I am. I am doing something for *myself* tonight. I am buying a new snow shovel because my family needs one. I hope that is an okay thing to do."

Well, Sam had the look about him that said, "My bishop's cup runneth over, and if I'm not careful, I'm going to drown in the flood of human foible."

So I said to him one Tuesday, "I have some time off this week. I have blocked out two days." In saying so I felt as though I had just cast my line into a fine, still lake, early in the morning, on one of those days when mist rises off the water as the sun peeps over the edge of the basin, when the lake is dark, except for the surface, which welcomes the warmth of the sunlight. There the fly sat, dainty, deceptive, and tantalizing.

Sam said, "Two days off? Planning anything?"

The fish had risen to take a look at the fly.

I said, "Oh, I don't know. I could stay around the house and putter and get some things done that Helen has been nagging me about. Or I could go fishing, I suppose."

Sam looked hopeful. "Fishing? You might go fishing?"

The fish was darting toward the fly.

"I was thinking about Snow Lakes Basin. It is a difficult

hike to get there and not for a casual fisherman, but it is where I think I might go."

Sam said, "Snow Lakes Basin. I've heard about it. They say the fish up there are monstrous. I've never been to Snow Lakes Basin."

Now, the fish had taken the bait, and all I had to do was set the hook.

I said, "Yes, they are big fish. I haven't been there in years, but I caught some dandy fish up there when I was younger. I guess I could go. The chores can wait." I paused, then said slyly, "Any chance that you could go with me?"

He wiggled with excitement and said, "Yes, I think there is a good chance of that happening. It might be nice to get away from things for a few days. Yes, it might be nice." The hook was set.

I said, "We will be better men and better priesthood bearers if we go fishing in Snow Lakes Basin. You will be a better bishop. You cannot be in such a beautiful place and not feel closer to God. It is not possible. Even an atheist could preach a fine sermon at a place like Snow Lakes Basin."

That is how our trip to Snow Lakes Basin began.

I have been on many trips to the mountains with Sam, and we have many stories to tell about our adventures, but other than our final trip to the mountains, when the thunder and lightning played like a symphony and tried to set afire rock and water and Sam caught his very last fish, we have never had a trip as memorable as the one to Snow Lakes Basin.

It is not easy to get to Snow Lakes Basin.

You drive more than three hours from our town on a road that twists through the mountains and follows the course of many streams. Then you get to a dirt road far away from anywhere and turn east and drive another dozen miles, through foothills cloaked in sagebrush and aspen, climbing higher, until you reach the pine country. The tree stands are thick, and you cannot see much, except the dirt road and the pines, and an occasional meadow, and the small stream that eagerly rushes to join a faraway ocean. But you are climbing in elevation, and you know that there are mountains through the trees, tall mountains, the mountains that cradle snow in hidden bowls and basins, even in July. The road ends in a pretty little meadow, and that is where you camp. But you are still a long way away from Snow Lakes Basin.

Sam and I made that part of the trip on Wednesday, starting late in the afternoon, so that we would have Thursday morning to make the remainder of our ascent. Before leaving home, we listened to the practical and sound advice of our wives about eating right, being careful, and not doing anything too foolish.

Sam and I listened to them with respect and patience, knowing full well that giving the lecture was their duty and hearing it was our duty, but that once we got into the car, all bets were off. We knew we would most likely do several foolish things on our trip to the mountains. I imagine motherly Sariah giving Nephi and her other sons the same kind of talk when they went back to town for the plates of brass, and then they still went ahead and did a lot of risky things. But, of course, Nephi had faith and the Lord was with him, so everything turned out okay. Still, when he explained to his mother the part about whacking off Laban's head, dressing up in his clothes, commanding the servant to fetch the plates, and then running like lightning to get away, Sariah could very well have exclaimed, "You did *what!*" and then gotten a very bad headache.

So this tension between the genders, when males are heading out on an adventure, has probably gone on a long time and probably will continue until the Millennium and maybe even after. I think Brigham Young would agree with me on this point.

Well, Sam and I got in the car and headed toward the mountains, which always brings a certain kind of fine pleasure and excitement. We talked about Snow Lakes Basin and the big fish we would catch, and I could see much of the bishop's burden seeping out of him. We stopped for a big mint milkshake at a little town called Stanley, the last outpost before we left behind anything akin to civilization. Just beyond Stanley we turned onto the dirt road and drove to where it ended and set up our camp, just as the sun dipped behind a craggy peak that reminded me of a gnarled hand with four fingers. The air was cold, and although it was summer, we could see our breath as we conversed in the light of the campfire.

"How big do you suppose the fish are up there?" Sam asked.

"They are big fish. Even though the lake is high and fish usually don't get very big at that elevation, so few people ever make it back in there that the fish in the deep part of the lake grow very large. I'm sure I caught an eighteen-incher on my last trip. Could've been twenty."

Sam's eyes sparkled as we sat across from each other, enjoying our small fire, eating gingersnaps and sipping root beer, a combination we never would have been able to pull off at home.

"Twenty inches. Wow. They are big fish."

"And they taste good. It's amazing that a creature that

eats mostly insects can taste so good. And that last fish might have been twenty-one inches."

"Yes, it is amazing."

We retired to our sleeping bags that night with visions of trophy lake trout dancing in our heads.

In my lifetime I have caught many fish. When I was younger I always put them in my creel, cleaned them, and ate them. It gave me great pride to come home and share my catch with neighbors, although now I'm not sure how much some of them really enjoyed receiving a squishy plastic bag with a dead fish with its head cut off in it.

But a few years back, I began to wonder about fish. I began to feel as though they were my friends. Although I freely confess to talking with trees, listening to mountains, and deciphering whatever other messages the land tells me, it is with hesitation that I write about fish being my friends, for fear that some people will think I have completely lost my marbles. I think I have kept only a half-dozen or so of the fish I have caught in the last fifteen years. All the others I have turned loose, usually with a word of encouragement.

"Good-bye, fish. Thank you for your time. I hope I did not frighten you too much. Better head to a deep pool now, and I hope you've learned the difference between a real bug and a bunch of feathers tied up to a barbed steel shank."

And since, according to scripture, all things have a spirit, I wonder if the time will come in the next life when I'll sit around and somehow communicate with all the fish I've caught through the years. I hope they're not upset with me. I hope they say to me, their little fish lips moving, "Oh, it's okay, Marcus. When I came to the earth, I knew that I might end up in a frying pan, in a pool of lemon butter, with my head lopped off. I was actually relieved when you clubbed me with the rock to put me out of my misery. Man, I can't believe how stupid I was to mistake a royal wulff fly for a real mayfly. That was really dumb. But don't worry. All is forgiven."

Then we'll sit around and talk and relive the experiences, and the term "fish story" will take on a whole new meaning.

Sometimes, when I think of the possibilities of universes yet unknown and yet unexplored that are awaiting us, I get so excited that I can hardly stand it. I hope I never lose my natural curiosity and that my imagination burns throughout the eternities like a new star, even if that occasionally leads me to conversations with resurrected fish, which, I acknowledge, is out of the ordinary. But if our ultimate aim is to be, in the most sacred sense of the word, creators, it seems to me that an imagination will be crucial to our success.

The following morning Sam and I rose before sunrise and assembled our fishing gear. Our plan was to hike the six miles into Snow Lakes Basin, fish, then return to our base camp that evening. On Friday we would fish a nearby stream that poured out of another chain of lakes to the south. Then, on Saturday, we would come home with big fish for our family and friends. We left our camp without a thought or care, since in those days, you could leave behind all your gear and not worry about someone stealing it. We left just after sunrise, with light hearts and high hopes.

The trail rose gradually for the first few miles, but it was enough of a grade for both Sam and me to get a little winded, and we rested occasionally. I kept my eye on the ridge we would need to cross to get to Snow Lakes Basin.

As we got closer to it, I kept having the thought, *That ridge looks steeper than you remembered it, Marcus.*

The trail eventually turned south, but the ridge was to the north, so Sam and I set out cross-country, our eyes focused on a small saddle in the ridge, where we would cross. We soon stood at the base of the ridge, and looked at it. The top of the ridge was a good 700 feet above us, and it looked like a nasty hike to reach it.

Sam said, "That's quite a climb."

I said, "Yes, it is. It is steeper than I remembered." And I was concerned because a ridge is always even steeper than it looks.

Sam said, "Lots of shale. Footing will be bad. We could slip."

I said, "Yes, we could slip. It would be a long fall."

He said, "There is an avalanche chute up there on the left. We could follow it up and use the bigger rocks for footholds. I also see some small trees we could grab hold of. Then we could scramble across the face of the ridge and push to the top."

I said, "You're right. We could. The rest of the ridge is bald, but those trees might come in handy. Still, it is a climb with some risk."

We studied the mountainside before us, calculating the risk and the energy it would take for us to get to the top of the ridge. And then Sam said, "Twenty-inch trout?"

"Twenty-inch trout. Maybe twenty-two."

And then we both looked at each other and said, "Let's go."

So we began the arduous journey up. It took us more than three hours to travel what was not much more than a quarter-mile, and my legs felt like wet, limp spaghetti, and my arms turned to rubber, and my breath came in huge, deep gulps. My hands were scraped and cut from grabbing so many sharp rocks in the avalanche chute. I was soaked with perspiration and more than once thought it would be nice to turn around and go back to camp.

But in the mountains, as in life, you cannot always turn around and go back. You must live with your decision and the consequences it brings. As anyone who has spent time in the mountains knows, it is often more difficult and dangerous to go down a steep slope than continue to climb up it, especially when the footing is bad. So there was no turning back for Sam and me. We kept our eyes not on the top of the ridge, our destination—and certainly not down to the alpine valley from which we had ascended—but only on the next step we had to take. That is often the best way to deal with a difficult journey, I have decided.

Every few minutes we would stop and wait for the pounding in our chests to subside and to feel a strand of strength return to our arms and legs. We were physically drained, too exhausted to talk, inching our way painfully up the mountainside.

Finally we had only a few dozen feet to go; our struggle was almost over. Knowing we were that close to the finish, we gained strength and our spirits lifted. Sam arrived on top first. When I got close enough, he reached down, gave me his hand, and pulled me toward him. I stood next to him on the windy ridge top. All around us were mountains, four separate ranges, each solemn, glorious, and beautiful. If Sam had told me that we were standing at the center of our universe, I would have believed him. Drained though I was, I stood there, more than 10,000 feet high, and thought, *The journey was worth the effort.*

And to the north, in their basin, laid out like four

crystal-blue diamonds, were the Snow Lakes, two of them, the ones in the shadows of mountains, still caked in ice.

We sipped water and ate some trail mix and rested for a long time. The hike down to the lakes was tricky; more talus slopes, steep, and a snowfield to negotiate. I was not eager to hike again, but I was eager to fish.

"The fish await us," I finally said. "Twenty-two inchers. No, probably twenty-four inches. Maybe bigger."

Sam pulled himself up from the curve of the rock where he rested. "Let's be on our way. This is going to be a bear to get out of tonight. We are wasting time that could be used for fishing. Have you ever caught a twenty-five-inch fish?"

It took us nearly another two hours to get to the bottom of the basin. It was now mid-afternoon, and something nagged at me, although I pushed aside whatever the vague feeling was that bothered me. The lakes were before us. We got not our second wind but our third or fourth. Sam and I eagerly pulled our light packs off and rigged our fishing gear. That is what we had come for.

Sam always fished with a dry fly. He considered anyone who fished with bait as belonging to a lower caste of sportsman. He was a man of unfailing patience and tolerance, but I heard him once mumble, when sighting a fellow fisherman threading a worm onto a hook, a one-word condemnation, "Philistine."

I never did tell him that when I was younger, I had occasionally fished with worms. I viewed it as a youthful indiscretion, but I knew it would be a test of our friendship and wished not to risk it.

I loved watching Sam fish. The flicking of his wrist, the rocking of his arm, the tip of his rod bending so slightly, the wavy line above his head, the whizzing sound of his line splitting the air, the dual look of deep concentration and supreme satisfaction. He could place his fly wherever he wanted, and his fly always landed gently on the water, just nicking the surface, never with a splash, but purposefully, as daintily as a woman's tear falling on a flower. It all worked together so well: the passionate energy of the long line curving in big smooth ovals as he cast, and the still, flawless point where fly met water.

It seemed that time stood still at that instant, when Sam's fishing fly skimmed and delicately settled sweetly on the water. It was like a baby's kiss. He was that good.

Sam found a place to fish, in the darker part of the lake just out of the shadows, the crumbling wall of a mountain behind him. I walked to another part of the lake, stepped over the small stream that bled from it, and settled at the end of a small finger of land. Monstrous fish, I told myself. Monstrous fish are in there, and they are hungry, and you and Sam are here with your rods in hand, and life could not be much better.

Well, there may have been monstrous fish in the lake, but they had decided they weren't hungry just then, and Sam and I fished and fished for almost two hours, and we caught only a couple of ten-inchers, both of which we tossed back. The wind skipped down the ridge line and teased the water, causing it to ripple and lap against the shore, turning the water into honeycombs of amber. Wind is not a friend to a fisherman high in the mountains.

We had been working back toward each other and finally were in easy talking range.

Sam said, "So this is Snow Lakes Basin, home to trout the size of Moby Dick, and so far all we have to show for it is two tiny fish that we tossed back. It is a beautiful place, but I want to catch a big fish. I worked too hard to get in here." He rested his rod on the ground as he tied another fly to the end of his line.

"The fishing will pick up. When the sun drops behind the ridge, the fishing will get better. The wind will stop, the lake will become still, and the fish will start biting. You have little faith, Sam. And you a bishop."

When I said, ". . . the sun drops behind the ridge," it occurred to me what was troubling my mind. It had taken us four hours to get into the basin, and we had left almost all our gear back at camp. If we started back to camp in the next hour, we would still arrive at nightfall. A later departure, and we would make part of the trek in darkness. When given the choice, I would much rather walk in light than walk in darkness.

"We can fish for another hour, Sam, and then we'd better head back. We can fish Washington Lake and some nearby creeks tomorrow, an easy hike from camp, although we might not have it to ourselves," I said. "More people congregate at places that are easy to get to."

"Okay. I would like to climb out a little more to the west than where we came in, though. There is another saddle on the ridgeline, and I think it looks like an easier hike from here."

He nodded toward the ridge, and I could see the place he spoke of. In fact, I had noticed it also on our trip in, and wondered if it would be an easier way out. Having grown exhausted climbing over the ridge to get in, I was not eager to grow even more exhausted climbing out, especially if we were losing daylight and we had no fish to show for our efforts. Scrambling down over talus would be risky, too. I did not want to climb out the way we had climbed in. In this case, the easier way out was also the better way out.

"An hour. Let's just fish another hour," he said. "We can

walk in the dark a little way. It will be almost flat the last mile. I brought my flashlight."

I said, "Okay. One more hour."

I looked around the lake and the mountains and gazed toward the sky. It is always an interesting rivalry to me, this gentle contest between land and sky to see which dominates. The brawny land with its mountains and trees and water is beautiful, but in the end, the sky that is the dome to all that takes place on our earth, always changing yet always the same, triumphs because it is large beyond our comprehension and we must always look up to see it. It is home to the sun and the stars, and I believe, the Father and the Son. That is why I think the sky is ruler over all the elements.

One hour later, the sun was dipping behind the ridge in the dark blue sky, and I was getting ready to call out to Sam and say we'd better head back. But the unseen hand that had pushed the wind all afternoon took a rest. Suddenly the lake was gray and still, but mostly just still.

Except for the fish that began to turn, nipping at the mosquitoes above the lake's surface.

Sam grew excited and looked more intense than he had all day. Here was proof that fish, some of them big indeed, resided in the waters of Snow Lakes Basin. I got caught up in the fever, too, and cast my line with renewed excitement.

For a few moments I forgot the waning sun and the mountains and the approaching collision of night and day.

I soon caught my first good fish, about fourteen inches long, and slipped it into my creel. A few minutes later, casting from a rock that rose twenty feet above the lake, I caught my second keeper, slightly larger than the first one.

Then I turned toward Sam and watched him. For twenty years or more, I had witnessed his uncanny ability to know where the fish were. His old Boy Scouts always said Brother Nicholson could think like a fish, and through the years I had come to believe it myself. He read water as if it were a book. Sam perched on some smaller rocks at the edge of the lake, near where the stream swept away, sending water down the basin on the first step of a journey that would end in the Pacific Ocean. It was not a place where I would have chosen to fish because the water was not very deep, and the shadows were dark and purple on the current.

But then, I never claimed to know what a fish was thinking.

Sam's line suddenly pulled straight, his rod bowed down, his back rose perpendicular to the ground. A furious thrashing began thirty feet away from him, and I could tell that it was a very big fish.

Sam pulled his line, coaxing the unwilling fish toward shore, watching it flip and spin and fight over every pebble. He worked it patiently toward the shore, inches at a time, and finally reached down and pulled the line. He grabbed the fish in his left hand and deftly worked the hook out of its mouth with his right hand.

And at that moment, with the sun working its way up the shale mountainside, painting it an earthy pink, the placid violet lake at my feet, the sky racing toward a midnight blue, I understood why I have been fascinated by fishing my entire life.

The cold barb of experience yanks us from our home waters, where we are happy and comfortable, into an atmosphere foreign and uncertain, one in which we can suffocate. And we whirl and writhe and pour out our fury at what we cannot see and cannot understand because we are frightened and cannot recognize a larger plan. And in the end, we hope it is a kind and gentle hand that takes away the painful steel hook and gently returns us to our home, and we are scarred, but alive, and wiser for the experience.

I thought it true then and still think it true now. I cannot mistake the parallel. It is the meaning of fishing to me.

Sam held up his prize fish, easily eighteen inches or more. Grinning, he slipped it into his creel.

The lake waters were dark now, the shadows moving steadily up the craggy, cracked wall of the mountain. "We need to go now!" I cupped my hands and shouted.

"Okay, okay," he shouted back. Then Sam cast again.

I watched him for another minute, then broke down my rod and put it in the carrying tube and stuffed it into my small day pack.

I walked closer to Sam and again shouted. "I am going to try to hike out now. Catch up with me!"

As much as Sam loved fishing, he would not allow me to climb alone on an unknown slope, which, I suppose, is one of the marks of a true friend. Reluctantly, he hauled in his line and said, "Wait a minute. I'll go with you." He then wound in his line, took apart his rod, put it in its tube, and lashed the gear onto his small pack. He walked to me slowly. "I know there are other big fish in there. I know that. I could have caught more. The fish are lucky tonight. But we do need to get back to camp."

Our prospects of getting back to camp were growing darker by the minute. We set off at a brisk pace, staring up at the ridge above us, a sense of urgency in our movements. We scrambled up the first couple of hundred feet, panting, perspiring, searching for good handholds and footholds. The ridge was not as difficult as the one we had climbed earlier in the day, but our light was being swept away, and everything was taking on the mottled gray color of dusk in the mountains. It became more difficult to see where we were going. Our pace slowed, and it took us another thirty minutes to travel the next one hundred feet. Neither of us said it, but we knew we would not get back to camp that night.

In my creel the two fish wiggled and gasped one last time, though they had been caught more than an hour earlier.

Finally, with only the pale light of a yellow moon to guide us, we reached the top of the ridge. The evening wind swept up the slope, chilling us, and I shivered. My legs and arms were weak, my breath coming in short gasps.

We gazed down into the little alpine valley, which was dark and cozy. Yet I knew we would go no farther that night.

I said, "I think this is the place."

Sam said, "Yes. I'm afraid so. Our wives always tell us to never do anything foolish when we go to the mountains, and we almost always do. We should listen more often to our wives. They are wise, wiser than we are. How can we be blinded by a few fish? I don't know about us, Marcus. I just don't know."

I said, "Yes. We should listen more to our wives. Let's not tell them about this. They will make fun of us and never let us go to the mountains again."

Sam said, "Deal."

I said, without conviction, "Do you think we should try to get a little farther?"

He said, "No. We can't see what is below us. We could stumble or fall. We may have to jump, and it is never wise to jump in the mountains, especially at night."

I said, "My father taught me that. Never jump where

the footing is unsure. We need to drop back over the ridge a little. I noticed a narrow ledge and a small dead tree. We could build a fire to help keep us warm. And we would be sheltered from the wind."

He said, "It sounds like home. For a night. Maybe we can find a stick and put our fish on it and cook ourselves a little dinner."

So that's what we did. We climbed back down the ridge to the rock ledge. We found some twigs and branches and broke the dead tree into chunks. I was glad that I always carried matches in my fishing vest, though I never had need of them, until that night.

We had both packed sweatshirts in our day packs, and I was relieved that we at least had had the sense to do that. We found a long branch, cut and sharpened it with a knife, and used it as a skewer. Wishing for some salt, we cooked our fish and drank what little water we had left in our canteens. Then we settled in for a long, cold night, trying to get comfortable on a rock ledge, in a place we should not have been. That night taught me that it is difficult to feel comfortable when you are in a place you should not be.

The only real danger we faced was that we would be cold, miserable, embarrassed, and not get much sleep, all of which happened.

We were not, however, alone.

The stars began to appear. Subtly at first, faint winking points of light on a deep blue canvas. As the evening turned fully into night, the dark velvet sky deepened, and more stars appeared, and their magnificence grew. Some blazed. Some twinkled. Some shot across the night, impossibly fast, impossibly beautiful.

I looked for Orion and his bright brother stars, Rigel and Betelgeuse, even though I knew it would be a few more months before he began his nightly hunt. Sometimes I look for things even when I know they are not there.

Moonlight rippled across the Snow Lakes beneath us.

And when the gentle breeze grew weary and blew itself out, the silence was complete, other than the hissing of our little fire and the sound of my own beating heart.

Late, very late, perhaps a little after three in the morning, I managed to doze. My next recollection was of Sam, standing, a black silhouette against the horizon eastward, glowing in pink and amber.

I watched him for a moment; then I stood. I ached and wondered at what point my body had turned to stone in the night.

"Good morning, Sam."

"Same to you, Marcus. It appears that we made it through the long evening. Weren't those stars exquisite last night?"

"Yes, they were. Let's climb to the top of the ridge and see if we can get down to the other side. What I want most in life right now is to get warm, fall into my sleeping bag, and not be disturbed for a few hours. Call it my own plate of pottage."

"A good plan. I don't even care if we fish again on this trip. You will never hear me say that again, Marcus. Never. It seems almost a repudiation of my religious beliefs."

"And since we ate your big fish, we do not even have a trophy to show for it."

He shrugged. "At least I'm only a little hungry. The fish gave his life for a good cause: our well-being."

We gathered our gear and stretched a little and rubbed our eyes and yawned a dozen times more. I was tired, dirty, and felt as though my joints were fashioned of hard cold ice. Then the full sun reached our ridge, and my shivering stopped for the first time in many hours. Below us the lakes were dark and mysterious. Sam started up the ridge. I said to the lakes, "This time the triumph is yours. We will leave you alone. You are most splendid in your cold isolation."

In only a few minutes we reached the top of the ridge. Sam said, "Look."

Directly below us the ridge dropped off a good forty feet. The drop was sheer and dangerous. Loose gravel, the most treacherous footing of all, littered the steep slope. In the murky night light, we could not see nor tell how precipitous the cliff was. Had we proceeded in the dark, had we dared to jump where we could not see clearly, we almost certainly would have fallen many hundred feet. I remembered again the words of my father, "Never jump in the mountains, Marcus. Never jump to a place you cannot see."

Sam said, a wry expression on his face, with a hint of relief, "Maybe our home on the ridge last night wasn't so bad. Cold, but not bad."

We trudged another quarter-mile along the ridge and found a safer place to descend. We had to find our way back to camp over a second, but smaller, ridge line to the south. We got back in early afternoon, and I have never been so happy to see my old, warm sleeping bag.

Sam and I had vowed to never let the details of our night on the mountain be known, but through the weeks and months that followed, little pieces of information gradually became common knowledge among our family members. Perhaps it was better to divulge a morsel of information here and there because it took a while for Helen and Ruth to get the full picture. Generally they would just shake their heads and cluck their tongues and say something underneath their breath about men and mountains and foolishness. So overall we got off without too much chastisement, although I once heard Helen tell Ruth that when it came to men and fishing, it was difficult to tell who had the more highly developed brain, the men or the fish.

Of course, the answer to that is clear to any fisherman and any fisherman's wife. The fish, generally speaking, are much smarter.

In Ruth's kitchen, I rose from where I was sitting, close to her sink.

"It is a very good story," I said, after I finished telling it to her.

"Yes, it is. We laugh about it now. But I suppose it wasn't too funny at the time."

"No, it wasn't. Stories change. Stories almost always get better when we have the time and understanding to look back at them," I said. "The passage of time allows us to interpret them and apply what wisdom we've gained. Experiences have many layers. That was the coldest night of my life, though. That part will never change."

"And what you said just now. What you told me about why you like to fish. How did you say it? 'The cold steel barb of experience' or something like that? You see so much sometimes, Marcus, in things that are all around."

I said to Ruth, who looked as though she was thinking hard, "But here is a way that story has changed. At the time I thought a kind and gentle hand could only turn the fish back to the lake."

She said, "What do you mean?"

I said, "Now I know differently. Sometimes it is the kindest and gentlest of hands that takes away and does not return the living thing."

Ruth said nothing. But the look on her face told me that she knew. She was thinking of fish and lakes and times gone by and times yet to come. She was thinking of her Sam and how a kind and gentle hand had taken him away and how, for at least a long, dark, and cold evening, she stood alone on a ridge, with only the moon and stars and a dark lake to keep her company.

And how the elements all conspired to create silence, not noise, and the beating of her heart was all Ruth could hear.

The gentle hand that takes away.

Ruth knew. She knew.

Chapter Seven

The remainder of the day slips by, no more stories to add to my collection. Then it becomes Sunday, dark and cold outside but as of yet no sign of the snow that I had expected. I turn to the clock next to my bed. It is not quite six, yet I know that I am probably awake for the day unless the speaker in church happens to be particularly dry, in which case, I might exercise my old high priest's prerogative and close my eyes during sacrament meeting.

Like most Latter-day Saints, I have come to know and treasure the rhythm of the Sabbath.

It begins with first wakefulness, the drowsy gray search through the mind, and the consciousness that Sunday has arrived.

It takes shape with the recollection of the day's coming events: lessons that need a final touch; talks that need practicing one more time; the anticipation of greeting friends, brothers and sisters, outside the chapel.

It progresses to the gentle cadence of the bishop clicking on the lights of the church in the still, morning hours; the familiar timbre of the organ; the restrained gait of Primary children, arms folded, earnest, as they practice reverence while walking toward their classrooms.

It is marked by higher thoughts and quiet revelation; a small cup of water and bit of broken bread; a prayer for someone who weeps or mourns or is lost; and the never-ending silent pleas to heal our brokenness.

And if all goes well, it ends with a feeling of sweet peace and the quiet assurance that God is near and that we will do little things better because salvation comes from the small things we do.

That is the way of Sabbath days, kept holy, by honest hearts.

I lie there, still, for another hour, watching the light filter into the room. Helen stirs.

"Are you awake?" she asks.

"Yes, I am. I have been for quite a while."

"You never did sleep well on Sundays. Too many early morning meetings through the years. Your body clock knows when it is Sunday. A terrible condition to find yourself in, I imagine."

"Well, we need to get up and get started anyway. Church in two hours, and we don't move as quickly as we once did. How families with young children manage is a weekly miracle."

"Young children . . ." Helen's voice trails away.

"What about young children?"

"Last week we sat behind the Pearsons, and you made faces at their children, and I think Melanie was almost ready to ask you to leave her family alone. Marcus, you cannot tease or make faces at the children in the ward. It sets them off. Honestly, you need to act your age. I never dreamed that when we were in our seventies, we'd be having a discussion such as this."

Part of being a male, and more than that, a male who holds the priesthood, is to sometimes simply accept defeat gracefully at the hand of his spouse, especially when the evidence is overwhelmingly against him. Yes, I had flirted with four-year-old Sarah Pearson and her two-year-old sister, Hannah, through a good portion of sacrament meeting last week. But the speaker had wandered, and I didn't think anyone other than the two blonde-haired sisters with dimples the size of dimes had noticed I needed a diversion. I was being proven wrong on this particular point, however.

So I said to Helen, "I am sorry. I will try not to be a disruptive influence again in sacrament meeting."

"Well, someday those sisters might come in to see you for a patriarchal blessing, and they might recall the times you teased them in sacrament meeting."

Actually, that thought hadn't occurred to me, and when Helen said it, I must admit I rather enjoyed the notion of pronouncing a patriarchal blessing upon someone whom I had teased and flirted with in sacrament meeting when she was a little girl. I tried to sound repentant, but was probably not convincing, because you can only repent when your heart is in it.

"I will try to do better."

Helen said, "I know you, Marcus." But her voice was light, and I flattered myself that what she was really thinking was, *I married this man in the temple. We are sealed. If everything works out right, we will be together a long time and then some. I'd best get used to his quirks. And, anyway, I kind of like his quirks.*

At least I hoped that was what she was thinking.

Helen sat up in bed. "It is different now, these Sunday mornings. All those years of getting three girls ready for church. Now I just have myself. I used to dread those days when you were in meetings, and the girls and I had to get to church on our own, but now I kind of miss those times. I would like to return to them."

I said, "Are you sure? Would you really want to go back and go through all the things we have experienced?"

She said, "I don't know. Sometimes I think so, but I'm really not sure. Maybe for just a visit."

My head was still on my pillow, and I stared toward the ceiling as the morning light gathered and ushered away the dreary gray around us. For many days now, I had been thinking of stories and gathering stories and, so far, had sought them only of my daughters and Ruth. For reasons that I could not fully explain, I hesitated to ask the same of the person who knew me best on the earth, the woman with whom I had shared almost fifty years of my life. I wondered, would she, because she knew me so well, too clearly understand why I was seeking these stories? Would she hear the rustling of those dry leaves sweeping across our landscape, and would she know, would she understand, precisely why I had set out to gather these stories?

If so, it would cause her pain.

And I would never willingly put Helen in any kind of pain.

Yet her stories may be the ones I most need to hear.

And does she not, after all these years of marriage, have the right to tell the stories of our life together?

Yes, she does.

And a moment of revelation struck. I thought, *They are the stories of our life together, not of my life alone. Our stories are too intertwined to be separate.* And the phrase from the Doctrine and Covenants, grammatically incorrect, spiritually perfect, coming after the discourse on the new and everlasting covenant, made sense to me: "This is eternal lives." For a moment, just a moment, fleeting and bright, I grasped the meaning of oneness in the sealing ordinance and the multitude of eternities. And in that moment,

Helen's stories became my stories. I would ask her, and hope that she would not understand my motive.

I picked up our conversation again, fishing for a story. "What has been the best part of your life? What would you like to do over or do for the first time?"

She looked at me and said nothing for a few seconds. She pulled the covers higher on her. The furnace clicked on, a low, comforting rumble.

Then she said, "I will draw a picture of it. The girls are young. We are outside, in a place like a park, but not a park, a place we have never been before. There is a meadow. The girls have on bright dresses and black patent leather shoes. Their hair is long, and they are happy and laughing. Maybe we are there on a picnic. You are there also. You are dressed in a blue suit and a white shirt with a new red tie. You look so very handsome, Marcus. I am there too, dressed nicely, taking the food from our picnic basket and spreading it before us.

"It is a warm day, only a few puffy white clouds. I will put some mountains in my picture for you, Marcus, mountains behind the meadow where we are, because you would like to be close to the mountains.

"Then we would hear music. Sweet music, music from a flute or a violin or both. You would take our little daughters by their hands and dance with them in a big circle in the meadow. It would be so delightful for me to watch. We would be young again, Marcus, and time would have no hold on us."

I turned my head toward her. Helen was looking at the window, now bathed in early morning light. She seemed to be in that meadow at that moment.

"If I could create a world for us, that would be it. But only for a time. I guess we can't go back and probably really don't want to. But what a time our moment would be."

I sat up and reached for Helen's hand and tenderly clasped it in mine and remembered the scripture that says only man counts time.

"Dancing with our daughters in a meadow. It is a true picture, Helen, and I can see it, and it is beautiful. Dancing in a slow, sweet circle."

I remembered talking with Sam once, in his backyard, as he practiced his golf swing. Sam had buckets of plastic golf balls with little holes in them, and he would turn the buckets upside down and scatter the golf balls and pull out his clubs and hit them from his yard into his neighbor's yard, the Marcums.

The Marcums were fine people, who didn't mind the little plastic golf balls being hit into their yard because Sam always picked them up, or sometimes, he'd invite the Marcum kids to catch the golf balls, and pay them a nickel for each one they caught on the fly. All in all, it was a nice arrangement: Sam polished his golf game, the Marcum children earned a little money, and it was a very pleasant way to spend a soft, warm spring evening.

Anyway, I heard the click of the club and the whizzing sound of the plastic golf balls as I was walking through the neighborhood, and I strolled into Sam's backyard, to stand behind him, at the edge of his garage, so that he didn't see me.

He looked very happy, and the Marcum kids were out trying to catch the plastic balls, shouting and pushing and laughing and generally enjoying life. I was taken by the moment; it was a scene of true charm, which doesn't happen often in our life, but when it does, children are usually a part of it.

Eventually Sam turned and saw me, and he greeted me, and we made small talk for a while, and I always stopped talking just as he went into his stance. I'm not quite sure how we got on the topic, but we ended up in a serious conversation, talking about how good our lives were and how blessed we felt. The incident is further evidence to me that one can have lofty, pure, and perhaps even holy thoughts while holding a golf club in his hand. The two activities are not necessarily mutually exclusive.

We got to a point where I said, "Sam, what is the best part of life then? What would you put your finger on?" The conversation Helen and I were having reminded me of what Sam had said.

He rested the head of his seven iron on the ground and lightly leaned on the shaft, thinking hard. Then he said, "Everything."

I said, "Everything? You mean as in *everything*, all things, the whole ball of wax? Good times, bad times, and whatever else falls between?"

And he said, "Yes, everything." Then he gripped his seven iron and took his stance and launched another plastic ball, sending it on a high, whirring arc against the blue of the springtime sky, propelling the Marcum children into another frantic chase.

I have thought about his answer through the years. I do not believe it was flippant, nor do I think it just rolled off his tongue. I believe that Sam had thought about it and truly meant it. Everything. Simply everything. Sam understood life. He was the happiest man I have known, and I think that was part of his secret. He found something to like, enjoy, learn from, or laugh at in every situation. And so I think his answer was a reasoned, intelligent one. In his own way, Sam was saying to me what Helen had just said: He, too, had danced in a slow, sweet circle.

I turned to Helen and said, in a room now brighter with morning light, "That picture. That picture of the meadow. It is our slow, sweet circle. It is. I know it."

She looked at me and just said, "Yes." No more needed to be spoken. So we stayed there, together, for another half hour, and talked about our girls and held on to each other and held on to the vision of a meadow and a mountain and five people named Hathaway in the sunlight of a warm early summer afternoon.

We were old enough to know that you can only hold on to anything, or anyone, for just so long.

CHAPTER EIGHT

I was good in church that day. Oh, I teased and flirted with a few children but only between meetings, when it was okay to do so. I sat in my place on the hard, wood bench with the thin cloth cover and didn't wiggle much. I did not get up during sacrament meeting for a drink of water, and I think Helen was pleased, overall, with my behavior. In Sunday School class, I answered a couple of questions and didn't bring up anything to contradict what the instructor said, although at one time I almost quoted Brigham Young to the class, and another time I thought about throwing in a zinger from Hugh Nibley to help with the flow of the discussion. But I resisted the temptation to do so on both occasions.

I even enjoyed the lesson in high priests group, so all in all, it was a fine Sunday at church, and the day was made better by the prospect of Betsy and Mark coming by for dessert that evening.

Betsy and Mark have been married a little less than a year. Mark is also a school teacher, and he met Betsy at one of those singles conferences, a meeting that Betsy was loath to attend. At the time, Betsy was thirty-two and had never married.

"I don't know why I go to those things. I never meet anyone," she complained.

"Why don't you go just to hear good talks and good

music and maybe make a new friend or two? Are those reasons not enough?"

And she looked at me in much the way her mother does occasionally, a simple glance consisting of about equal parts pity, amazement, and vexation that seem to say in one brittle word, "Men."

But on this occasion she went, and a couple of days later told her mother that she had met a nice man who was divorced and that they were going out together. Mark and Betsy dated for about six months, but we heard very little about the course of their relationship, until one brisk, clear autumn evening when Besty said that Mark wanted to talk to me, and I knew it wasn't to ask about my golf game.

So he came in, and I did what most good, though overprotective LDS fathers do. I roughed him up a bit by letting him know that one of the principles I held true was that no man on the face of the earth was good enough for any of my daughters. But, I finally conceded, if marriage was mutually agreeable to both parties, I supposed I could go along with the notion, although I wasn't wild about the idea.

During my ramblings to him, Mark had a look on his face that said, "You are kidding, Brother Hathaway. *Aren't you?*" And when he left the den a half hour later, he still didn't quite know what to make of me and my answer, which is just about the way I wanted things.

I guess I'll need to repent for the whole episode, and I probably will. Someday.

Well, Mark and Betsy were married and sealed, and I must confess that I started to warm up to him a little. He treated our Betsy so well. He was kind, sweet, and considerate, and perhaps a little naïve, but in a nice kind of way. He was not a man who needed to count things to be happy.

In fact, I wished that some of him would rub off on Quinn, and perhaps it still will. I also recognized that Mark is a complicated young man, with a strong desire to *do* right and not necessarily *be* right, which is as the equation should be.

He also plays golf, though not very well. When we played last in August, I took him by nine strokes, and it has something to do with the male ego, but his losing to me actually earned him a few more points in my book.

I do not know the whole of the circumstance of his first marriage. I am certain the pain still runs deep, and details may come out someday, but we will not ask anything.

Mark also brought two little children into our lives, Erica and Cassie, and when I see him with a daughter in one hand and cradling his baby in the other arm, I feel happy, envious, reminiscent, satisfied, and anxious all at once. I do not know how to explain this mixture of powerful emotions, other than lessons I know from the mountains: freshets and brooks, streams and rivers, and oceans are all connected and all join together, and so are we in our families.

So we had some pie and ice cream, and Helen apologized for buying the pie from a store, but no one cared. It was fun to have a part of my family in our home and to hear little girls laugh. Plus, warm pie and vanilla ice cream constitute one of life's great pleasures.

I hope that if Mark and Betsy have a child, the baby will be a girl and that I will be able to watch their three girls and see new meanings in my three maple trees.

After the pie, Mark played on the floor with Erica and Cassie, and I went into the kitchen to help with the dishes. Betsy followed me in and grabbed a dish towel. We have an automatic dishwasher, but sometimes it feels good to dip your hands in warm, sudsy water, and hand the dish to a person next to you to dry. It is a wonderful time to talk, to the comfortable rhythm of washing and wiping dishes.

Betsy looked at me, a little slyly, and said, "I have another story to tell you."

"Another story? This is an unexpected but very welcome event."

"Well, it's not much of a story. And it took place less than a year ago, so I don't know if it really has all the trappings of a good story because time seems to give stories their final shape and meaning."

It pleased me that Betsy said that. It told me that she had also thought about stories and used them to navigate through life. Perhaps Betsy would be the storyteller of the next generation of the Hathaway family.

She wiped dry a plate. She wiped it so hard that it squeaked.

"The story comes from the day Mark and I married. It has to do with a phone call and the wise and practical advice that my father gave me. Do you remember?"

Yes, I remembered. I would always remember. It was too funny to forget.

Betsy and Mark had an unusual courtship. It was not love at first sight, and even more than a year later, I'm still not quite sure it is love between a man and a woman in the traditional sense, but I am firm in my conviction that it is headed that way. They were both wary, Mark because he had been torn and scarred by his first marriage, and Betsy because she was well past what I suppose our LDS society thinks is a "respectable" age to wed. In their hearts, I think they both wanted to love and be loved, to give freely and without fear, but because of their backgrounds, both needed assurances first.

A relationship is a delicate balance of heart and mind, desires and needs, hopes and fears, fragility and iron wills. What phantoms must have convulsed in Betsy's and Mark's minds when, late at night, they tried to think and talk things through!

It sounds odd, but to me their courtship in some ways resembled the early rounds of a boxing match—each of them now and then throwing a tentative jab, dancing in the ring a bit, falling into an occasional embrace, sorting their way through their opponent's defenses, and pausing periodically for a dejected retreat to their respective corners. More than once, one or the other had to take a standing eight-count before the match could be resumed.

But it had all worked out, and on that night in early November, when Mark stopped by our home, nervously cleared his throat, lost most of the color in his face, and croaked, "May I speak to you, Brother Hathaway? Alone? And soon?" I knew that we would be involved in a wedding in the near future.

And the near future it was. They checked their school schedules and decided that a week before Christmas would be the perfect time for the ceremony.

Helen, to her everlasting credit, merely smiled serenely and said, "Yes. Of course we can work on the wedding and get it all taken care of in the next few weeks," although inwardly, I knew she was thinking, *Not right before Christmas. A springtime wedding would be so lovely.*

So the wedding took place in December, and though I liked Mark well enough, and, of course, loved my daughter more than I can begin to explain, a little part of me still worried about them.

Then when the sealer in the temple asked Betsy and Mark to look into the mirrors that faced each other on the walls of the room and asked them what they saw, and Mark said simply, "Eternities," the Holy Ghost enveloped me and said, "Don't worry, Marcus, all will be well, and this is the way it is supposed to be." I thanked Him silently, and have not had a worry about my Betsy and her Mark and their daughters since.

It was also a time of sadness for me, in perhaps a way that only a Latter-day Saint can imagine. This is a simplification, but I feel it is true. I think each of us was given a list of things that we would need to do, or at least try as hard as we could, to accomplish on the earth. Little boxes to check off, I suppose. Brigham Young said that we receive knowledge "a little here, a little there," and I wonder if "here" means earth and "there" means other worlds. I suppose the time comes when we've learned all that we need to on earth, so we are called back home to learn things that are better taught elsewhere. At the temple last December, I felt another box had been checked, one of the very last boxes, by witnessing our youngest child sealed. I thought, *Maybe there is only one box left, and that is to endure to the end.* Life's great events—births, baptisms, priesthood ordinations, missions, and marriages—all serve as markers along the road. And they also remind us of our own mortality. It was probably more than coincidence that I started noticing the scurrying of leaves about the time of Betsy's wedding last year, and what was once only a nagging malaise, now seems an urgent siren to my soul. I see the road of Marcus Hathaway coming to a canyon that cannot be avoided. Brigham Young said, "How dark this valley is! How mysterious is this road, and we have got to travel it alone."

Then he said, "this dark shadow and valley is so

trifling," explaining that when we cross it, we won't think it a big deal, and in fact, will look upon the experience as perhaps the highlight of our whole existence.

Well, when you go to the temple, and you see the things of eternity happening there, and the Spirit is thorough in His presence, you tend to grow introspective, which is what I did that day.

The remainder of the day was a blur. A wedding luncheon followed, then a reception, and it was a nice reception, nothing too fancy, simple food, no long receiving line, just the bride and groom and the parents. And when it was all over, we had quite a mess to clean up, but I was glad for family and friends who pitched in.

It was a little before midnight when Helen and I were finally slumped onto a couch at home, trying to recover from the day's events, when the telephone rang. Helen moaned but rose wearily and picked up the receiver.

I heard her say, "Oh, hello. I'm surprised to hear from you. Is everything well, dear? Good, that's good."

She was silent for a moment, then Helen said, "Oh. That is unusual."

It occurred to me that she was talking to our newlywed daughter. I thought, *We have taught Betsy to be gracious, and maybe she is calling to say thanks for everything.*

Then Helen said, "I don't understand that. Not at all. It makes no sense to me." Her tone was rather grave.

And I thought, *Maybe they have the jitters. It would be okay to have the jitters and would be entirely understandable. They'll need to work things out. I hope it's just the jitters.*

Then Helen said, "That's nonsense. Completely. What is wrong with Mark?"

And I thought, *Maybe it's a case of* extreme *jitters.*

Helen said, "I'm going to put your father on the

phone, and you can talk with him, and then if it still doesn't seem right, I'll have him talk with your *husband*."

And the way she said "husband" was cause for concern. She said the word as though she were choking down a tablespoon of bitter medicine.

Then I began to feel sorry for myself. If it were a case of the jitters, even extreme wedding-night jitters, I did not want to be the one to get on the phone and do some coaching. I was seventy-three years old and much preferred to let nature take its course in this instance. But Helen looked exasperated and disgusted and was walking over to me with the cordless phone in her hand.

She commanded, "Talk with her. And maybe him."

I had no choice.

I said, "Hello, honey. How are things going?"

She said, "Hi, Daddy. I guess things are okay. But I'm confused about something."

Helen stood close by me, her arms crossed, her foot tapping.

There are times in a man's life when experience and good sense shout to him, "Be careful about what you say next. When a daughter on her wedding night calls and says she is confused, it is one of those times. You don't need to be very smart to understand that. A lot is riding on your choice of words." So I gulped and said, "In what way?"

Betsy hesitated.

"Go on, sweetheart. Is this about the jitters?"

I thought I heard a faint laugh, and I was relieved, but only a little.

She said, "No, Daddy. Not really. Maybe a little. See, BYU has a football game."

I remembered that. A bowl game in Hawaii. A time

difference of three hours. My mind jumped ahead. The game must be late in the third quarter.

"Yes. A football game," I said, feeling woefully inadequate as a patriarch. I wondered what wise Helaman or strong Mormon would have said.

"Well . . ." and her voice lowered to a whisper. "Mark is watching the football game. He wants to watch the football game. That's what he wants to do right now. He says it is almost over."

"And you had another vision of tonight?" I said, which was not a very bright thing to say. I imagined Helaman and Mormon shaking their heads and saying, "Brother Hathaway really doesn't quite have it all down yet."

"Yes," Betsy answered. "Yes, as a matter of fact. Do you blame me?"

Helen looked at me as though I were responsible for the situation, as well as for every other weakness and foible demonstrated by members of my gender throughout the ages.

I thought, *Somehow, maybe this is all my fault. We males have to help each other out more than we do. That is what the priesthood is supposed to be about. Brotherhood and service. Mark needs to work on the brotherhood part a bit more.*

Betsy said, "Well? What should I do?"

I spoke slowly and hoped I was being wise. "Do you have a BYU sweatshirt? You were going to the coast after this. It's cold there in December. Did you take a sweatshirt that has BYU written on it?"

Betsy said, "I did. I have it. It's somewhere in my suitcase."

"Then I suggest that you change your clothes, put on your sweatshirt that says 'BYU' on it, sit down on the bed next to your husband, and cheer on the Cougars. Besides, they don't have much of a defense this year and could use some support."

A silence followed on the phone. A long silence. Then Betsy said, "Okay. I'll do just that. Tell mother good-night and that I'm sorry I interrupted. Good grief, Daddy."

"It's fine, Betsy. We love you. Good-night. Oh. And what's the score?"

"BYU is down by seven, but they have the ball."

"Sweet dreams, my darling Betsy."

I hung up and faced Helen.

"You told her to put on a BYU sweatshirt and watch the game with him?"

"I did."

She let that piece of information sink in. Then she came over and sat down beside me. After a moment she said, "It's probably good advice."

"It was the best I could do."

She leaned over and kissed me and rubbed my mostly bald head. "You're a practical man, Marcus Hathaway. Maddeningly practical sometimes."

Well, BYU lost the game anyway, and I was kind of glad about it. Mark and Betsy came home a few days later, and the incident had not been mentioned again until now, although I'm sure it will come up around the dinner table occasionally and probably be handed down for a generation or two more. Even fifty years from now, Mark will blush when the story is told, and everyone will have a good laugh. Our stories define us through the years.

Betsy, indeed, was smiling as she recounted the story, while she finished drying the last of the dishes. "It was good advice, Daddy. I suppose marriage requires you to adjust and overlook some things. Maybe a lot of things on certain occasions."

"Yes, it does."

At that moment Mark came into the kitchen and said, "Better get home now, Betsy. Lots to do to get ready for tomorrow. And I wouldn't mind watching the last part of the Seattle game, if that's okay with you."

He looked at Betsy, then at me.

"What? Did I say something funny?"

Two hours later, I was still smiling.

CHAPTER NINE

Monday came, cold, foggy, as thick and laden as a Wagner symphony. It was a day designed for pulling the covers a little higher around the neck, turning away from the face of the clock, and dozing a little longer. Helen stirred, rose, and began her day.

I had retired early, before ten o'clock, but I still felt fatigued. I closed my eyes again. Then Helen was leaning over me. "Marcus. Are you all right? It's past nine in the morning. Are you okay?"

I was groggy. "Yes. I'm tired, that's all. Just tired."

"When we get back from Seattle, I want you to have a physical. A complete physical. I don't want you to walk into Dr. Rose's office and talk to him about golf and distract him and trick him so that he gives you a light exam. I want everything looked at, from your toes to the top of your head."

It was easier to surrender, and probably more prudent. "Okay. But I'm just tired. I'll get up in a few minutes."

Almost a half hour later, I rose and prepared for the morning. Helen had already started to pack her suitcase and had half of my clothes laid on the bed when I finished showering. We were going to Seattle on Tuesday to celebrate Thanksgiving a week early with our eldest daughter, Kate, her husband, Rob, and their six children.

And it would be with all six children. Twin sons, Marcus

and Samuel, would be arriving home on Wednesday and Thursday, from their missions in Scotland and Argentina.

We will go to the airport on Wednesday afternoon and greet Marcus, then return on Thursday evening for Samuel. Much has changed since the two brothers left on their missions. Their grandfather Sam passed away about four months into their service, and a year later their family moved from Ann Arbor to Seattle. Rob is a medical researcher, and when the university there offered him a responsible new job, he took it. So Marcus and Samuel will be returning to a new and different place.

Through the years I have enjoyed watching missionaries return. When they leave they are almost always equal parts enthusiasm and trepidation, not quite sure what they are getting themselves into, simply exercising their faith that all will turn out well and that the Lord will not ask them to scale a mountain higher than they are able to climb. They know they will miss family and friends, good food, a comfortable home, and someone who will do their laundry for them. They often struggle at their missionary sacrament meeting, trying to sound profound and spiritual, trying to prove they are ready to join the Lord's army—hoping to persuade the congregation to forget how they had had to repeat the sacrament prayer three times only last April and to dispel the rumor that when they got cut from the varsity basketball team eighteen months before, they had gone home and cried for an hour.

Through the dispensations the Lord has called upon, trusted, and loved people who were not quite ready for the assignment they were given, from fishermen in Galilee to young men in white shirts who slipped a name tag onto their new suit coat pocket and began to answer to the call of "Elder," and then shipped out to a place often very foreign and perhaps bereft of physical comfort.

I've imagined that more prayers are offered on behalf of those young men and young women than just about any other category of people for whom we pray. More than for the sick and afflicted, more than for the prophet, more than for bishops or stake presidents. That's the way it should be. When one of our young serves a mission, mothers and fathers, sisters and brothers, grandparents and friends are also, in a way, called to serve. We all pray, we all fast, we all mark the slow days, one by one, until our tired elder or sister takes the sweet steps through the passenger gate at the air terminal and falls into the embraces of those who missed them the most.

The gospel, I have often thought, teaches us so much about farewells and journeys and homecomings and trusting that all will be well when we arrive at our destinations. It is the way of learning about faith.

And when our missionaries return home, if they have served to the best of their ability and learned all that they should have, it is written on their radiant faces and imprinted on their souls. They have glimpsed the eternities and for a moment understood where they stand and known where they ought to go.

So it is with great anticipation that one tired old grandfather will board an airplane tomorrow, accompanied by a silent, strong hope that somewhere in the airport lobby later in the week, amid the tears and pure, chaotic joy that he will have the chance to hug his grandsons and say, "Well done, Elder. We missed you. Welcome home."

It is probably the closest thing we will experience on this earth to the reunion of the Father and the Son when the Savior's mission on earth was completed. I am only sorry that my true friend Sam will not be at the airport with us, to also greet his grandsons, but I suppose if a layer or two of the veil were peeled away, we would see him at our side, pleased and smiling.

So I begin to pack my suitcase, with the vision of a glorious reunion in my heart. Our flight is not until late tomorrow afternoon, so there is plenty of time to prepare, although I think everything is checked off. I have asked a friend from high priests group, Morgan Gardner, to be my crossing guard substitute.

As the day wears on, I still feel tired; and shortly after lunch I lie down again, my breath coming in short, shallow, little puffs. I doze again until it is dark.

Outside, just before I fall asleep, the wind kicks up, its whooshing sound jarring the house.

I do not need to even glance at my three trees in the backyard to know the last of their autumn leaves have fluttered to the ground.

The light of my grandsons' return dims in the brooding gloom. I feel it is winter, somber winter, in a world growing dark.

CHAPTER TEN

Helen is worried. Her eyes show it, her voice tells it, and the light lines on her face seem more furrowed.

"You slept so much today, dear. Should we run you in to the hospital? Don't let the trip worry you. They will get along fine without us at the airport. I called Kate this afternoon and said you weren't feeling well. She said everything would be on videotape and we need not worry about greeting the boys."

"But I'm fine, Helen. Sometimes I just need a little extra rest. That's all. Brigham Young said men should rest more when they're young because they'll need the energy when they are older. I should have heeded his advice. I worked too hard."

She looks dubiously at me.

I try to squelch her worries by taking a huge bite of my baked potato. For some reason, watching a man eat a large meal always has a calming influence on women. "This is a good potato. May I have some more salad dressing?" I say, trying to distract her and cheer her.

"Yes, certainly," she says, but the worry is still in her voice.

"It's only that I'm tired. But I feel better now."

She takes a small bite. It is dark outside. The sun never punched through the clouds. In the late afternoon, after the wind had stirred, a huge, slate-gray cloud covered our world and had begun hurling little icy snowflakes at us. Our back porch light is on, and I can see their hard round shapes bouncing across our patio. The wind slaps the side of our home, and an apple tree that I planted too close to our house many years ago scratches at the siding.

"Could be nasty weather for our trip tomorrow. I hope not. I do not like to fly when I can't see the mountains and the ground and the rivers and the trees. I'd like to see Mt. Rainier. I hear it is beautiful, and sometimes the pilots get very close to it," I say between bites. "I like to read the land."

Helen stood up and turned toward the sink. She said, "The girls have told me something. Betsy and Debra. They have told me you have asked them to tell you stories. I don't want to talk about Mt. Rainier, Marcus. I had a feeling about what you told me on Sunday. I want to know why you are asking our daughters to tell you stories. I love your stories, only this time, I fear your stories, or fear why you are asking they be told."

Her back was turned away. Her shoulders slumped. She reached for a sponge and scrubbed the sink with something close to anger. What could I say? Should I have told Helen about leaves and autumn and the coming winter and what I hear and what I feel? Was it disingenuous of me not to include her, not to ask her about the stories of my life—no, *our* lives? For a moment I felt selfish and a bit of a fraud. Why the masquerade? The woman I've known for fifty years. How could any story of my life be told or be complete without her?

Then came a cleansing thought from Sunday. *Because you did not want to hurt her. You did not want to hurt Helen.* And I grasped hold of it because I knew, beneath my quest for stories, beneath the rough texture of my entire earthly experience, there was a fine and tender part of me that did not want to risk hurting her. Perhaps not a wise decision on my part, this exclusion of my wife, but one made with sweet intentions.

She raised her head up and stared out the window. Were it daylight, she would be able to see the three bare trees. But it was now too dark to do so.

And I thought of my answer to her, and it was a good answer because it was true. I said, "You know why I am asking. You know. I just wanted to hear the stories that will be told of me. I'm sorry if it is wrong and maybe sorry that I didn't tell you my whole motive on Sunday. I'm sorry if it hurt you. I didn't mean to. I only meant to spare you pain."

My throat felt heavy, and fatigue washed over me again. Then I said in a small voice, "Helen Hathaway, it would do me great honor to hear the stories you would tell of your husband."

She turned slowly toward me. She looked thoughtful and composed. She walked toward me, and I stood and took her in my arms. She said, "There is only one story, Marcus. It is the story of the two of us, from the beginning till now and from now until the end, and the end will never come for us. That is the story, and it includes everything— our children, who we are, what we've done, who we have become through the years. It is that simple and that complex. I can't say it or think it any differently. I love you, Marcus. I'm sorry if that story was not good enough or too short for you."

I held her close and said, "It was a fine story. It is the best story. It is the only story I ever would want to hear from you."

I don't know how long we stood there. But in that time,

I felt our story, clear and true. Sometimes we tell stories, sometimes we listen to stories, but the best stories of all are those that are felt. We do not always need words to express what we feel.

We are taught from the time we are in Primary that we come to earth to gain a body and learn all we can, because knowledge is the only thing we can take with us. But I think that equation doesn't balance. Knowledge may not even be the most important thing we acquire. Wisdom comes before knowledge, and before wisdom, our relationship with others. Everything else pales when compared to relationships, the friends we have, the feelings for our family, the greatness of our love for one another.

And in that time, when Helen and I stood there holding each other, with that fine thought, when the night finally succeeded and absorbed the light around us, I saw something every time I closed my eyes.

A meadow, with a mountain nearby. A pretty young woman with dark hair, a picnic blanket spread upon the grass. A man, almost handsome, in a blue suit and a red tie. Three little girls in white and red and yellow dresses. Music from a flute, then a violin. And all of them holding hands and dancing in a wide, slow, sweet circle.

Chapter Eleven

With sunrise came a surprise.

Fall had put on a new face, much different than the brooding, dark one we had seen yesterday.

A clear, cold blue sky, the hue of an ocean on a summer morning, greeted us. The mountains northward wore a new shawl of snow. The blazing depth of the sky, the dazzling white of the snow, the subdued green where the snow line met the forest on the mountain, all combined to uplift my spirits. The day spoke to me, a voice mature and comforting: Marcus, we are perfect in our seasons, part of a wise, blue autumn.

And of course, I would see Kate and Rob this day and before the end of the week, my grandsons, now almost returned missionaries. When I arose, it was with a hopefulness about things to come.

I still felt tired, but soon after breakfast, I went to the garage and found my bamboo rake tucked in the corner. I told Helen, "I need to rake up the last of the leaves. It will only take me a few minutes. I will feel better leaving our home knowing the leaves are all raked up."

She said, "There are only a few. They will blow away while we are gone. Why not stay inside, Marcus, and make sure everything is ready for the trip?"

She didn't understand what the falling leaves had come to signify in my life. I didn't expect her to. Helen saw me raking leaves; I saw myself as confronting a fear. Better to confront our fears than live with them and allow them to haunt us. Better to face what the leaves represent than to let them blow wild through my life.

Soon after lunch Helen said, "It's time. Debra will be here to take us to the airport, Marcus." In Helen's mind we could never get to the airport too early.

"Okay. I am ready. I'll get the suitcases and move them to the front porch."

"I checked with Ruth, and she'll be fine. I asked Betsy to call her, and I'm sure Marcy will check in on her also. Marcy has been so good to her mom. She checks on her every day."

"Well, let's go then. Debra just pulled up in her nice car. We'll go in style."

I carried the suitcases to the car, greeted and kissed my daughter, who also seemed in good spirits. "I'm jealous. Sam and Marcus are my first two nephews. Give them a big hug for me. I wish they could all come back next week for Thanksgiving. What a day that would be for our family!"

We climbed into the car. "The airport, please, driver," I said. "Get us there on time, and there may be something in it for you."

"Will you pay for any traffic tickets?"

"Certainly. And I may even come out of retirement and be your legal counsel, should you require it."

With that she slapped her foot on the accelerator and we squealed out of our cul-de-sac. I looked back at my home, the place I had lived for more than thirty years, and felt a longing that I could have explained but chose not to. We turned the corner, and my home disappeared. There was no time for good-byes from a man who talks to mountains, fish, lakes, and trees, and who would have liked to have spoken to his house.

The skies stayed sunny, and as I had hoped, the pilot flew close to the north shoulder of Mt. Rainier. I studied it, searching for alpine lakes and canyons that scraped down its side. I knew that this mountain and all mountains were where waters collected and became creeks and streams, and I enjoyed seeing the birthplace of things important to me. Even Helen, who does not enjoy flying, seemed calm and happy on this trip, flipping through magazine pages and occasionally glancing out the window, looking at the chain of Cascade Mountains stretching southward—massive Rainier, shy Adams, broken St. Helens, and spindly Hood.

And I was happy at that moment, with beautiful mountains seemingly close enough to touch just outside my window, my wife at my side, and reality of a sweet family reunion only a short time away.

It was also at that moment that I felt a stabbing pain run from the left part of my chest up and over my shoulder and jolt down my back. Breathing came in quick, shallow bursts.

Helen noticed my quick gasp when the first bolt of searing pain shot through me. "Are you okay, Marcus?"

"I am fine, Helen. Just sitting too long in this position. But look. Do you not agree the world is beautiful and glorious?"

She nodded and smiled and took my hand in hers. The pain almost went away.

The airplane made a wide looping turn to the north, and we began our descent. Clouds covered Seattle, and as we dropped in altitude, we were enveloped in a thick, cottony, gray cumulus soup.

Soon we were in the terminal, hugging our Kate, who seemed tired yet filled with energy. "I haven't slept much in three nights," she chattered. "Can you believe this? Two more days and I'll have my whole family home. *Home*," she said, and I could feel her exultation in the way she said the word. "I'm exhausted, but I don't want to miss anything. Not a thing. *Home*," she repeated. And she led us to the car, and soon we were driving on the freeway toward her house, just north of Seattle.

We had been to Kate and Rob's house only once since they moved at the beginning of the summer. Their home sat on the side of a hill, tall evergreen trees everywhere, with a view of a lake in the distance.

Standing on the front porch with our suitcase as Kate fumbled with her keys, I said, "Do you like living in Washington?"

Kate said, "Oh, yes. The summer was beautiful. It clouded up in early October, and we've hardly seen the sun since. But I don't mind, so far. The drizzle comforts me. I think I can get used to it. And the kids are doing fine now." Then she found her key and started to unlock the front door, but she stopped and turned around toward me and said something most remarkable.

"Look at our yard, Dad. There are no fallen leaves. Everything here is green. *There are no brown leaves.*"

Abruptly, she turned back to the door and flung it open. And she said again, "Everything here is so green. It's not like fall or winter here. Seasons take on a whole new meaning."

We walked into her house, and Helen took the obligatory tour to see how things had changed from our earlier visit, when most of the moving boxes had still been unpacked. I settled onto a small chair in Kate's family room. They came back in, and we spent an hour in conversation, catching up, finding out new details about each of our grandchildren. Kate's excitement at the prospect of her sons' return was palpable; her eyes shone, her conversation was animated, her laughter contagious.

Our grandchildren began to arrive home from school. The boys, Andrew and Nathan; the girls, Lindsay and Holly. Few feelings in the world compare to having a little boy or girl walk through the door, shout, "Grandpa!" and run and wrap his or her arms around your waist. Feeling the part of a patriarch comes, I think, not so much by age or priesthood office; rather, I think it comes when generations of family are around you and the love you feel is tangible and true. Then Rob walked through the doorway, and he hugged me, then Helen, and said, "It is so good to have you in our home, Mom and Dad." And we talked for another hour, and the gray outside began to thicken, and the drizzle turned to rain and tapped an uneven but soothing rhythm against the windowpanes.

Kate said, "It's almost six. I'm sorry, but I just didn't feel like cooking tonight. I called in an order for Chinese food. Anyone want to go with me to pick it up?"

I said, "I will. I would like to go pick up the food."

And Nathan and Holly quickly chimed, "We want to go with Grandpa."

So we bundled up against the damp chill and walked to the car, the yellow glow from Kate and Rob's home streaming across the lawn, children holding my hands.

A few minutes later we were at the restaurant, where the meal was not quite ready and a woman smiled and apologized, then apologized again, and asked us if we would be seated; then she apologized for the third time, and hurried back into the kitchen.

"The food is good here. It's worth the wait," Kate reassured me. Nathan and Holly stood transfixed in front of an aquarium with a blue light and lots of wavy plants and watched turquoise and orange and black fish undulate in the shadowy water.

"They come by it naturally," I said. "They get their fascination with fish from their mother."

"And where did I get it? All in the genetics, Dad."

"We had some good times, didn't we? Other than Sam, you may have been the finest fisherman I have ever known."

And it was true. Kate could read water, she could tell the size of a fish by the bubbles they sent up from the dark, calm water, she could match the right fly with what the fish were hungry for. If anyone in the next generational circle had the chance to think like a fish, it was our eldest daughter, Kate.

Then she surprised me, looking dreamy, looking content, still pretty, but with the first gray showing in her long brown hair. "Yes, we had some great times fishing. Do you remember when . . ."

Sometimes when people begin a sentence with "Do you remember when . . ." I worry because often now I do not remember when, and I feel as though a pair of hands is cradling my mind, keeping what I want to remember from emerging.

But when Kate said, "Do you remember when . . ." I felt no such anxiety. I knew that I would remember when. Kate was going to tell me of her first true fishing trip.

Another story. Another story for me to hear and remember.

It was in the early 1960s. Kate was ten years old. For weeks Sam and I had been planning a fishing trip to the Eagle Mountains in eastern Oregon, close to my boyhood home. I had not been to the Eagles for almost twenty years; it would be a trip fraught with good memories and fine times. Sam was going to take his sons, Rob and David, and for many nights, we would gather in one of our garages and plan our menus and check our gear and look at maps and talk about our trip and the many fish we would catch.

Some of those times Kate stood in one of the garages, near the door, not saying anything, which was unlike her. She just looked and listened.

Once I glanced at her, and she wore a long expression and seemed on the verge of tears. Then she turned and ran out of the garage, her sandals slapping the driveway. Rob, who in a dozen years would take that little pigtailed girl in overalls and sandals to the temple, looked at me and said, "What's wrong with her?"

And I said, "Oh, I think she is just going to miss her dad when we go fishing. That's all."

I told Helen of the experience later that night and how touched I was that Kate was already missing me, even though we would be gone for just five days.

Helen gave me a patronizing look and said, "Marcus, you flatter yourself."

"I do? And how do I flatter myself, if I may ask?"

Helen said, "She wants to go with you, Marcus. Don't you understand? Sometimes men just don't get it."

And to prove her point, I said something that fairly shouted, "Men don't get it." I said, "But she's a girl."

Helen, who had been in the backyard, picking the first

of the onions from our garden, put down her bowl on our kitchen counter with a little more emphasis than I thought necessary. "Marcus, just listen to me. You do not have to believe me, but try to. Kate wants to go with you. She loves the outdoors. You've promised her a fishing trip for years. Now she sees Rob, who is a little older than she, and David, who is younger than she, going on the trip, and she wants to go, too. Do you get it now?"

I decided the wisest course of action was to not say anything at this point but merely nod. So I nodded yes.

"Do you think you could take her? It would mean a lot to her."

I nodded yes again. I am a conservative man, when the times call for it.

"Are you not speaking to me because you are afraid of saying something else that you will regret?"

For the third time, I nodded.

"Then perhaps you should visit with Kate and invite her on the trip. And for heaven's sake, don't tell her that she will be the camp cook or the person to keep the tents clean. Teach her to fish, Marcus. Teach her to fish."

I nodded again; then feeling a little more bold, said, "Okay."

So I found Kate upstairs and asked her if she would come, and she tried not to look too eager, but said she would. I told her a little lie, that we had planned to invite her anyway but wanted to surprise her, which I don't think she believed, but children are the most forgiving members of the human race, which is a good thing for parents.

We included Kate in our plans from that point on, and I was careful not to make her feel as if she were to be the camp cook. In our backyard I showed her how to tie a leader on the line and a fly on the leader, and we practiced casting. I filled a tub of water and had her cast from different places in the yard, until she had a fairly good form, not too much arm, gently tossing the line in the rocking motion of the ten o'clock, two o'clock pattern. Once I put the tub of water under the three trees, which were in full bloom, because I thought she needed to learn how to cast under branches. I admit the number of trees and the number of fish I have snagged in my angling career are about equal.

A little less than two weeks later, we were off in the station wagon, Sam next to me as I drove, and Kate in the back seat, between Rob and David, and none of them seemingly very happy about the arrangement. The roads we took to reach our destination included a freeway, a state highway, a county road, and finally a dusty Forest Service two-track, which started in the sagebrush, climbed quickly into the pines, then dropped into the Eagle Creek watershed. We set up camp and ate chili and drank pop and sat around the campfire and watched as the sky turned orange, then purple, then a deep, thick blue, and stars began peppering the night, growing brighter as they continued their long spinning journey.

Kate wore an expression on her face that said, "All of this is somewhat interesting, but I don't understand everything about camping, nor do I care to. I came here to go fishing, and that's what I want to do."

I said to her, "Kate, we will get up at first light and go fishing. The fish bite in the morning and the evening, and in between they like to go into deep water and generally be lazy. So be ready when I wake you up."

She said to me, "I'll be ready."

And she was. Our tent was only a few yards from the creek, and the rush of dark water at first kept us awake, then lulled us to sleep. I have always enjoyed falling asleep to the sound of water in a hurry. The tumbling water also covered up the rumble of Sam's deep, sonorous snoring in his tent, two trees away. I wondered how Ruth ever got any sleep, and I expected Rob and David to be foggy-eyed and weary in the morning.

But at first light, when the tallest of the pine trees were easing from their slumbering gray and preparing to take on the shading of a fine, fresh green, Kate rose and shook me gently and said, "Let's go fishing, Dad."

We had apples and oatmeal for breakfast, washed down by watery cocoa. Sam and his boys were also up, and we silently got our gear ready. Finally, I put on my waders, looked at Kate, and said, "Let's go catch you a fish," and she squealed with excitement and picked up her rod and we marched down to the creek.

Sam, Rob, and David followed at a respectful distance as Kate and I walked up to fish the first hole.

"Now remember what I taught you. Remember the proper motion, not too wild, just a flick of the wrist, really. Always watch behind you for trees. Don't slap the water with the fly because it is just like telling a fish, 'Watch out, I'm here to get you to swallow my hook.' And remember that fish can see you, so never stand too close to the hole because fish by nature are skittish creatures, and they are fairly intelligent for a life form that has a brain the size of a small pea."

I said all these things with the best of intentions and realized that Kate wasn't hearing a word I spoke. Instead, she was looking at a place where the swift water clashed with a rock and at the still, deep pool behind it. She was reading water. Sometimes, I realized, you could be giving your children the best of all advice, the best your experience has to offer, lessons that you learned from difficult experiences, and it just doesn't matter. They have to experience it for themselves, even though you know you could save them some pain and make their life more pleasant.

So I said the only words that Kate would hear from me for a while. I said, "Go ahead, Kate. Drop your fly right on the top of the current and let it drift into that pool."

She drew her rod back, and the little fly on the end of it missed the trees behind her, darted forward, bolted back, moved over her head, slowed, and settled lightly on top of the water. It was a wonderful cast, a perfect cast, and I was stunned by the beauty of it and the surreal sense that a little girl standing at the edge of a stream, sunlight not yet brushing the bottom of the forest floor, had the power to make time stand still and the world take note of her by the way she flicked a rod and line and lure.

I wish I could say that an entranced trout saw the mayfly and rose to take it, but that was not the case. The fly drifted through the current untouched, braked itself against the boulder, and came to rest in the shallow backwater.

Perhaps the fish in the stream all knew what was going on, and paused in their carbonated, fizzy roil of water and air to look up and think, *What a nice cast by that little girl. Let's just watch. It is all so pretty.*

"Bravo! A natural!" boomed Sam behind me, and although he didn't mean to, he broke the spell of the moment. But I suppose moments such as those are not meant to last long anyway.

"Wonderful cast, Kate. You'll put all us gents to shame," I said.

Kate smiled and seemed to blush, although it was still dark at the edge of the creek. She pulled her fly in, blew on it as I had taught her, and cast again. The next cast was not nearly so perfect, nor the one after it.

I tried a few casts myself, with no luck. Sam and his boys fanned out ahead of us on the stream, and he promised to keep every other hole open and said he would occasionally just stop and wait for us as we fished. Sam and I always fished upstream in the belief that somehow our presence was telegraphed to the fish downstream through the flowing water, but not up, a kind of watery, one-way boulevard. Kate and I gradually worked our way along the east bank, casting and not catching anything and hardly getting a bite. The stars of the night had been accompanied by a friendly, full, pale yellow moon, which was beautiful to look at but which I figured made the fish indifferent.

My father had taught me that fishing after a full moon was futile because the fish could see the little bugs on the current better and fed more at night. His theory seemed to be true that day. After an hour I caught one fish, only ten inches long, and I debated about throwing him back but decided to keep him, on the chance that he was the only fish that we would catch. As he thrashed inside my creel, I could almost feel him gasping, and I felt a little bad about his pain, but I did not want to get skunked. Getting skunked as a fisherman is embarrassing—sort of like falling asleep on the stand during sacrament meeting and slipping off your chair and then making a loud exhaling noise while the speaker tries to keep his composure and the congregation is cracking up. Neither are things that you want to do if you can at all avoid it, and my ten-inch trout was my insurance that day.

Kate kept casting, some of them good casts, some of them slapping the water, and a few getting snagged in trees. I patiently untangled her line a few times, and she popped off a couple of flies on rocks, so I tied new ones on. Her initial enthusiasm was turning into grim determination as another hour went by and she still had no fish to show for her efforts.

We reached the waterfall. On East Eagle Creek there is a waterfall, maybe twenty feet high, and I don't know if it has a name or not, but everyone who has ever fished there knows exactly what you're talking about when you refer to "the waterfall." At the base of the waterfall is a deep pool of black water, and it is the best place to catch fish on the whole stream. When we arrived there, gentlemanly Sam and his sons called out, "Got any fish yet?"

I pointed to myself, then held up my index finger and mouthed the word, "One."

Sam shouted, "Let her fish the hole below the falls."

I shouted back, "Okay. She might get one there."

The problem was that the best part of the hole could only be reached from the other side of the stream. Were Kate to cast from the east side, trees would be in her way, she would have to drop her fly over a sizable stone, and the water was shallow. I needed to get Kate to the other side of the creek. She could go no farther from where she stood. She was too little for waders, and she could not cross the stream on her own.

I grabbed a smooth stick of wood that had washed up on the shore to use as a cane and instructed Kate, "I'm going to bend over. I want you to get on my back and put one arm around my neck and hold onto your rod with the other. I'm going to carry you piggyback across the creek, to a place where you most likely will catch your first fish ever."

I knelt down, and Kate climbed on my back. The water was swift below the pool, and I carefully poked my way across the stream, one slow step at a time. What normally would have been a one-minute crossing took five, but Kate and I finally reached the other side. I did not need to tell her what to do next.

She climbed up on a small rock to the side of the dark pool. She held her rod high and drew her arm back, slowly, rhythmically, the line and leader and fly splitting through the air, a faint zinging sound rising above the steady noise of the falls. She dropped her fly in just the right spot, and it floated there, dainty, deceptive, deadly. Sam leaned on a rock of his own across the creek, and his boys stood and stared, a mixture of curiosity and wonder in their eyes, because Kate was, after all, a girl.

Years later, after Rob and Kate had been married for better than a decade, I asked him when he first fell in love with Kate. He said, "When I saw her at the waterfall on East Eagle Creek. I knew then I would marry her someday, or at least that I would try to marry her someday, and that if I failed, I would be miserable. Funny, isn't it?"

A gentle back current actually carried the fly to the deepest part of a pool on the left side of where the water spilled over the ledge. I thought I saw a couple of bubbles rise, and my excitement seemed to boil over. Yes, a fish was down there. Yes, he was hungry. Yes, Kate's fly was there for the taking.

And take it he did.

The fish struck with a vengeance. Kate's rod arced to the water's surface. Her line zinged as the fish went deep. Sam and I and the boys all shouted instructions, but none of us were close enough to help. Instinctively, she pulled back on the rod and had the presence of mind to pull in some of her line. I'm not really sure what happened next because I was scrambling over the rocks to get to my Kate and her fish, but by the time I got there, the fish was flopping on a little rocky area in shallow water and Kate was excited and chattering and ordering us about all at the same time.

It was a good fish, thirteen, maybe fourteen inches long, black on top fading to a charcoal gray, with the thin slash of a red and green rainbow on his lower sides. I got to the fish first and held it in the air for her to admire; then I gently pulled the hook from his mouth.

Then the awful truth hit Kate about fishing. To catch and keep meant to kill, and though she had wanted to go fishing, she had not quite reconciled her tender heart with what it would mean when she caught one.

She looked up at me, her eyes filled with worry, and said, "Do we have to keep it? Can we put it back in the water?"

I said, "Yes, we can put it back in the water, honey, if that's what you want."

The fish wiggled and fought in my hands, gasping for breath. I squeezed it a little harder. "But I need to know now. Much longer, and it will die, even if we put it back in the water."

"Let's put it back." And then she said something that still brings me wonder. She said, "I want my first fish to live. I want to be able to think of him and when I do, think he is in the creek, still swimming around and still happy."

She was making, for perhaps the first time, the subtle connection between acceptable actions and unacceptable consequences, which is a link that some people, even adults, never fully understand. I admired Kate for recognizing that connection at a young age, and I saw a glimmer of the young woman and woman she was meant to become.

Across the stream and down the bank, Sam and Rob

and David were cheering and waving, and you'd have thought Kate had just pulled off a miracle of epic proportions by hooking a fish, and a decent sized one at that. I suppose neither of the boys ever looked at Kate as "only a girl" from that moment on.

I bent down and eased my grip on the frightened fish. I returned him to the cold waters, swayed him back and forth for a few seconds, then lifted my fingers. He was still for a moment and tilted toward one side, and I thought it might have been too late for him. But then with firm resolution, he righted himself, thrashed his tail with a keen and special fury, and darted back to the still, dark waters that were home.

I hope, more than thirty years later, he is still enjoying the bubble bath beneath the falls on East Eagle Creek.

Across the stream, Sam, Rob, and David stared, trying to comprehend what they had seen. At that time, it seemed that releasing a fish was contrary to a great unwritten code of the outdoors. I believe they later all came to a better understanding, but on that day, it was a mystery to them, one that they certainly talked over in their tent that night.

Kate would fish many times more. Only rarely would she keep a fish. "They're too pretty to catch and keep," she told me years later. "They seem perfect creatures in their own world and helpless in ours. They belong in the water. Don't you agree?" She taught me much, my Kate, when we went fishing. I hope to fish with her again, though I am too old now to ever wade in swift water.

We fished the remainder of the day, and Kate and I caught several more fish, all of which we released. I carried her on my back many times, crisscrossing the little creek, jack pine and yellow-dotted meadow at our sides, the china-blue hood of sky overhead. Sam and his sons did bring back a few fish, and together with my ten-incher, they made a nice dinner with boiled potatoes and canned fruit.

"Do you think it's wrong not to keep the fish?" Kate asked. "I think I like to fish, but catching fish isn't that important. Being where fish are is important."

"No. Don't worry. There is no right way or wrong way to fish. Everyone fishes in a different way, and the results are never the same," I said. "And we all fish in different ways for different reasons, and success means different things to different people. Some people keep fish, and some put them back. That's all."

Later that night, by the flicker of a feisty campfire, I pulled out a half-dozen flies and filed away their barbs. When we fished the next day, it was with no barbs on our hooks, making it easier for the fish we caught to find their way home.

Our Chinese food order was ready. The nice, apologetic hostess called our name, again said she was sorry, and smiled and handed us three large white bags filled with food.

"So what else do you remember about that day, Dad?" Kate asked, as we paid for the food, gathered the sacks, beckoned for Nathan and Holly, and walked into the chilly drizzle of a Seattle autumn night. The murky clouds hugged the earth and caressed it and moistened it, a fine dewy sheen coating everything.

"Not much more. Nothing really. Thirty-five years later and I'm still not sure I have made complete sense of that day and that trip. And what about you? What do you remember best?"

Kate scrunched up her nose, something she has done since she was a baby.

"One more thing. It's not much about fishing, really. It will surprise you, perhaps. Remember how you carried me on your back the rest of the day, and we got across the stream together many times? You were so patient. It meant so much." She paused as we approached the car, and she reached into a pocket and pulled out her keys. "You carried me. You remember the fish part best. I remember that you carried me."

I said, "It was a little thing. Any father would have."

She said, "No, it wasn't a little thing. Think about it."

I said, "What is there to think about? Only water that you could not have crossed alone."

She sighed as she reached to pick up the order of food that she had rested on the car's hood. "You are the one who sees so much in stories. Especially your fishing stories. I'm surprised you haven't thought of it. It's this, Daddy. I went as far as I could, and when I didn't have enough strength, you carried me. Do you see that? You carried me where I could not go alone. Across fast waters that would have swept me away. Over boulders that were too large for me to climb. You carried me."

She had lost me. I didn't understand the point she was trying to make. I felt old.

"So?"

"So this. We walk as far as we can, through difficult terrain, across swollen streams. Then, when we can walk no farther, He carries us. That's what I mean."

I said, "I know what you mean now."

Kate said, in the cool, moist night, "I understand you and your stories now. I've loved hearing you tell them all my life, but it has only been in the last year or so that I've

144

understood your stories, why you look for them, why you remember them, why you tell them. They carry us, too. Across dark waters. *We will tell new stories. There are more stories for us.*"

I thought much about her words as I spent a night surrounded by family. We told a few more stories, laughed together, and tried to not get too excited about young Marcus's return home the following afternoon, and Sam's on Thursday.

And at one time, with the fireplace blazing, the younger children on the floor, all of us listening to the stories and tales, the jokes and legends and fond remembrances, talking with tears brimming about the two boys who would be returning home in only a matter of hours, I thought, *Helen's vision of dancing in a slow, sweet circle is happening right now. It happens to us over and over again. We only need to see it.*

I fell asleep with pleasant thoughts of mountains and fishing, our girls little again, and contemplating the great wisdom of the night: We can dance in the slow, sweet circles as often as we choose.

CHAPTER TWELVE

My pleasant thoughts and good dreams do not last long. The pain in my chest and shoulder returns, first gnawing, then biting.

I awake. I think, *You ate spicy Chinese food. That is what the pain is all about.* I am still. I do not want to awaken Helen. I do not want to alter the plans of this day. Somewhere far to the east, Elder Marcus Nicholson is saying farewells to his mission president and his wife, hugging his companions, and boarding a plane. I want to will the pain in my chest to stop.

But it does not.

Breathing becomes more difficult. My lungs feel as though they are being squeezed. If I give it some time, the pain may go away. Yet my thoughts turn to the scraping of gray and brown leaves that has haunted me for weeks. Does it come to this?

The night sky seems to have cleared. Through the slants in the window blinds, I see the pale dead moon staring down, ghostly rays shining earthward.

The pain must go away. It can't remain. Not now. The timing is all wrong.

It is difficult for me to breathe. I feel clammy. I fight for each breath. I sense that my mind is not working clearly. I wish the elephant on my chest would rumble off to someplace else.

Each breath is agony.

If I get up, if I could only get up, maybe the searing, white-tipped pain would leave me. I turn slowly on my right side. With all the strength I can muster, I sit up in bed. The pain almost causes me to lose consciousness.

I stand up. I take two steps. My legs are weak, and I am gasping. The gray light of the room swirls about me in a dizzying pattern.

I sink to my knees. I am vaguely aware of the thud my body makes when it hits the bedroom floor. When my face touches the carpet, I feel some relief.

"Marcus? Marcus? Are you okay? What is it, dear?"

I cannot answer Helen.

"Marcus!"

She is leaning over me. I cannot speak. I want to tell her not to worry. I want to tell her that I love her. I want to say I'm sorry, so sorry, for things left undone, words not spoken, the things I could have done better. I want to tell her, too, that I tried hard in most whatever I did. All I can do is look into her face and fight to breathe and wonder why the tears stream from the corners of my eyes. I hurt.

Helpless. I feel so helpless. And foolish. Not on the day that young Marcus returns home. Not today. Not the day before Sam comes back from Argentina.

She stands up. I hear her cry for Rob and his urgent footsteps running down the hallway.

He rushes in, his face serious. He feels my pulse. He checks my airway. He rubs my forehead. Kate is right behind him.

"Call 9-1-1! Call now!" he instructs. "Okay, Dad, stay with us. Just stay with us. Please. Hold on, Dad."

He unbuttons my flannel pajamas. I feel his hands on my chest.

And then the agony diminishes. I close my eyes. Around me I feel a sense of movement.

Then light. Not a bright, overpowering light, but a pleasant, beckoning light. The excruciating pain dissolves. I want to think about the light. I want to move toward it.

The light is warm and inviting. It is the color of pearls. Everything is peaceful.

So this is what it is like, I think. *Brigham Young was right. Worrying about it was far worse than the actual experience.*

I cannot see, but sense, other beings nearby. I want to laugh and talk with them and hug them. My mother and my father. My eldest sister, Camilla, who passed away twenty-one years ago. Others are nearby. So pleasant. So fine. So peaceful.

And there is one more present.

Sam.

I think I should ask him how things are. I smile when I contemplate asking him if fishing is allowed and what the golf courses are like. I want to ask him if he's chanced on Brother Brigham yet, or Brother Joseph. I feel a sweet, blissful communication with those around me, though I see no faces, hear no voices, speak no words. Yet I understand they are close by. Layers of the veil have parted.

But what of my family?

I want to see my missionary grandsons again.

It is the presence of Sam I feel, again serving as my guide, as he has done so many times before. And the tender impression he leaves me is, "It is your choice, my dear friend, Marcus."

I smile again, a smile I can only sense. Of course it would be my choice. Agency again, our beautiful agency still prevails. How the Father and Son love it! But going back would be difficult. The pain in my chest is gone now, and I do not want to acquire it again. I also know I may be different if I choose to come back. These old ragged bodies of ours.

What to do?

What did Kate say? *There are no brown leaves. Everything here is green.* And later, *We will tell new stories. There are more stories for us.*

Yes, I think. *Yes, that is the answer.* In a time of need, as so often is the case, a family member provides the answer. Green leaves exist. I had only to look elsewhere for them. I saw only the leaves in my yard, the leaves from my trees. And my stories are not finished. There are new stories. Kate told me so. I want to hear them; I want to be a part of them. *My stories will save me. My slow, sweet circle is not closed.*

The beautiful, soft, opaque light dims a bit. I again feel the acute, overpowering pain slashing through my chest. Once more I hear Rob's voice, choked with tears. "Please, Dad. Oh, please, Dad. Please come back. Oh, please, dear Heavenly Father." I sense Helen and Kate at my side, too. I feel hands on my forehead and hear a distant, sweet, earnest priesthood blessing being spoken.

It will not be easy. I understand that. But I do not want them to worry. If I could talk with them, I would say, "It's okay. I have decided. I will not leave you yet. I have a season left. You will be pleased, I think. All is well. We have more stories to tell."

I am granted a vision: A deep blue marble of beautiful hue, swirled in white clouds, set against a vast and black canvas. I grow euphoric at the thought that it is the home of my wise mountains and vibrant streams, little fish and big fish, harbors with calm waters, family and friends for whom my love is boundless. Somewhere is a crossing guard talking to children and slipping candy into their small hands; and somewhere is swift water that can be crossed only with my help. Somewhere on that orbiting blue dot are my grandsons, and I want to see them again. Their return begins another story.

I am coming home.

I am coming home.